# The Haunted Man

## A Novel

by

## Alexander Raju

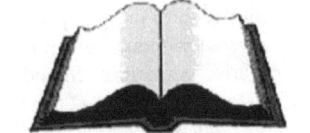

**CCB Publishing**
British Columbia, Canada

The Haunted Man: A Novel

Copyright ©2009 by Alexander Raju
ISBN-13   978-1-926585-22-2
Second Edition

Library and Archives Canada Cataloguing in Publication
Raju, Alexander, 1952-
The haunted man: a novel / written by Alexander Raju – 2nd Ed.
ISBN 978-1-926585-22-2
I. Title.
PR9499.4.R35H39 2009   823'.92   C2009-903277-5

Cover image, *Wanderer Above the Sea of Fog (1818)* by German artist
Caspar David Friedrich (1774-1840), is in the public domain.

First edition, 1997: Copyright ©1997 by Alexander Raju: Printed and published in
India, as Library Edition with a jacket designed by the author, by Dragon
Publications, Kottayam, Kerala, India.

Publisher:      CCB Publishing
                British Columbia, Canada
                www.ccbpublishing.com

*Dedicated to all the living and the dead victims
of the nineteen months' Emergency declared in India
at midnight on the twenty-fifth of June 1975.*

***Other works by Alexander Raju***

*Candles on the Altar* (1985)

*Ripples and Pebbles* (1989)

*Many Faces of Adam* (1991)

*The Psycho-Social Interface in British Fiction* (2000)

*Sprouts of Indignation* (2003)

*Magic Chasm* (2007)

*Upon This Bank and Shoal* (2008)

A score of centuries minus a quarter of a century after the death of Jesus Christ! And then...

He dissolved himself into a deep slumber, sucking the warmth of the creamy breasts of Goddess Mumbai. In that sound sleep, like a devotee who had achieved the bliss after a long and tedious pilgrimage, he pressed himself towards the mosaic floor which was as smooth as the bosom of the Goddess.

The platform! It was constantly receiving the tremor of the night trains that came in and out like the breaths of the Goddess! Goddess Mumbai, who never sleeps, had almost absorbed all the heat of the month of June into her fleshy chest!

His head swayed from side to side in that deep sleep as if seeking the rare particles of cold in the hot breasts of the Goddess. The hot wind coming like the sighs of the Goddess caressed his disheveled hair and tangled beard. And then, he was simply sleeping in mere oblivion, quite stoically like a wooden log!

He who had never dreamt all his life had been on his way to see and understand the real picture of his mother country. The journey which had begun from the groin of the mother, proceeded first towards the feet, from there to the breasts and to the head, then, along the left hand and, at last, come to a standstill at the right hand.

He curled himself into that corner of the first platform of the railway station, being too tired and exhausted by the day's worthless walk under the scorching heat of the summer sun. He kept his air-bag, and it was his sole possession, under his head like a pillow, and it was all puffed with his dirty, soiled clothes. The strap of that old canvas bag was clinging tightly to his neck as if it were afraid of platform pilferers!

For the last few days, he was staying on that platform, shifting every day the spot of sleep, without creating any suspicion among the railway police.

Even in that deep sleep, his mind was well-prepared to hear the noise of the sweepers who came to wash the first platform during the first hour of the day. When that noise resounded, his body would rise up from the first platform as if in somnambulism and would fall down in some corner of the second platform.

Later, at the fourth hour of the day, when the noise of the sweepers who came to wash the second platform resounded, his sleepwalking would be repeated. Again, reaching some damp corner of the first platform, he would sleep an hour more in utter forgetfulness.

When the fifth hour's electric train roared, he would wake up with a startle and walk away into the street, as if in another stretch of sleepwalking. By then, the batons of the railway police would have begun to tickle in between the rib bones of those who still were wearily sleeping on the platform!

He slept like an innocent child. Then, there was no reason

for him, as a person who had never dreamt, to be afraid of the hidden programs of fate. But, what was the state of affairs just before that sleep? Yes, just a few moments before he had begun his sleep, sticking himself to the bosom of Goddess Mumbai?

The ugly and distorted figure of the mother country had frightened him! The roaring laughs of the hunters who were trying to divide their own mother and to take the lion's share for themselves, had deafened his ears. The poor mother who had just been freed from the chains of slavery after a long meditation and a heavy bloodshed! The selfish deeds of the crazy power-seekers who were trying to keep for themselves the holy outcome of the sacrificial-fire into which thousands and thousands had let themselves fall like termite-flies, had nauseated him.

How many times had his hands itched to lock up in an iron box all the knowledge he had gained through years of constant efforts and hard work, and to throw away its only key into the wide mouth of the great ocean! But, then, he was quite indifferent. He was, then, ready even to suck the strong venom, had the breasts of Goddess Mumbai emitted the same!

As the railway clock struck twelve times, together with the chime resounded the noise of the sweepers who came with their buckets and broomsticks to wash the first platform. Such ear-breaking sounds that regularly echoed in the small hours of the day could not even frighten away the Goddess of Sleep!

Then, he too, as usual practice, joined other sleeping-fellows in their sleepwalking towards the second platform. In that somnambulism, everybody would forget whatever honor and prestige they had! And he also curled among those poor folks who received food, clothing and work only when miracles happened.

Yes! Miracle, though it is an everlasting truth, is always

unexpected and unknown! How could a person who had never dreamt expect any miracle? And that is why when miracles happened unexpectedly, he could only stand and stare at the truth in utter bewilderment.

While lying on the mosaic floor of the second platform, tucking the canvas-bag, filled with dirty clothes, under his head like a pillow, and as the light shifted from the figure '25' and fell on the figure '26' on the date slip that was placed on the table of the station master, he who had never dreamt in his life, glided into a dream for the first time. And he slowly drowned himself into the intoxication of that unexpected but wonderful experience. A miracle of a dream, a dream which was as true as truth itself...!

The immortal music of the flute...! It was flowing into the atmosphere and echoing and re-echoing everywhere! A cool breeze was blowing, spreading all over the earth the fragrance of wild flowers! Nature, forgetting herself, was disintegrating into that immortal lilt and tone of that music! And, according to that lilt and tone, the whole Yadava Clan was dancing with light steps, forgetting even their own existence...!

As the lilt and tone were progressing violently, the earth began to rise up and down and to turn round and round in a crazy rapture and intoxication! Slowly and gradually, the sea began to twist, turn and struggle, and to loosen the tides of huge, heaven-touching waves...!

The music of the flute was dissolving itself into that thundering roar of the waves and was slowly vanishing in that commotion. And the Arabian Sea, with a sudden convulsion of a tsunami, galloped up, gaped and swallowed the City of Dwaraka, the capital of the divine king of the Yadavas!

When those tired and exhausted waves returned to their abode, the sea was falling into a nap. Only the broken flute was searching for the Dark Singer among the rotten, stinking dead bodies of the Yadavas. Vultures hovered over the carcasses that returned to the seashore and were lying scattered here and there. Wolves howled quite ominously, roaming among those mangled dead bodies!

And when the wing-beats of the white vultures and the howling of the black wolves resounded in the atmosphere, Goddess Mumbai was sitting impassively and apathetically...!

At the end of that horrible dream, he felt that the city that never sleeps remained silent and inactive for a moment. And then...ah...then...?

Then, the sound of the horse-hooves falling on the road echoed everywhere in the street. Tlut...tlut...clop...clop...

The sound of the steel-soled shoes and boots of the soldiers and policemen silenced the waves of the Arabian Sea. His semi-conscious mind, that was only awaiting the usual noise of the sweepers who were coming to wash the second platform, trembled in the wavelets of the vanishing first-dream!

But, by then, those who were on the second platform began to yell and shriek like beasts and to run helter-skelter, like the frightened sheep all of a sudden finding wolves among the flock, as if they were escaping from an unexpected earthquake or an avalanche!

The steel-shoed boots threshed and trampled over the mosaic floor! The batons and canes of the soldiers and policemen were hissing over the heads of the fleeing masses. The breasts of Goddess Mumbai were crushed under their boots and her navel and pelvis were bruised under their batons!

And in the next moment itself, he too ran aimlessly

together with others who were madly plying away to nowhere! The cyclone that had blown heavily over the streets vanished suddenly, and it was, perhaps, hiding somewhere for a better opportunity! The dust and the miasma aroused by it gradually began to settle down.

But, even then, the shrieks of children, the sobbing of women and the yelling of men were echoing and reverberating throughout the streets. Those who had been sleeping on the footpaths were panicky over the loss of their women and children and they searched for them even in the dark, filthy water of the stinking, deep gutters!

The human worms! They were fleeing aimlessly without finding any hiding place or a hole to hoard their heads at least like the foolish ostriches!

Being incapable of finding out a way to console these poor souls who were punished most cruelly for their only crime of being born in this land, Goddess Mumbai was simply counting the waves of the Arabian Sea!

He cursed himself and aimlessly got into a train that was restlessly hooting to scurry away. Was his journey, which had begun with a clear purpose, at last reaching at utter aim-lessness?

His heart was turning hot and beating fast. Was this aimless journey the fate of all those who had never dreamt? Was this the punishment given by Time to all those who live without seeing dreams? If so, he could not accept such a fate! And his heart was burning and fast palpitating.

Was it not because he had tried occasionally, at least, to feel the true pulse of his mother country? But had not all those attempts turned even his very existence upside down?

He felt that the bosom of his country was quite cold and frozen. There, the blood that oozed out of her bruised nipples frightened him. What a pity, oh, Mother!

Alexander Raju

Then, he traveled to the head and there he distinguished the worms that writhed and foamed in her benumbed brain. From there, he traveled towards the feet and, at last, returned to the groin where he was born.

Mother had fallen down and was lying unconscious! He ran away being afraid of those vultures that were impatiently waiting in queue to tear away the flesh of Mother and those wolves that were standing with lolling tongues for their turn to break her bones!

The warmth of Mother's left hand aroused hopes in him for a moment. And from there, he went to the Himalayas where he wandered along the ranges in search of the Mrita Sanjeevani, the medicinal plant that gives life to the dead.

At last, sharpening his ears for the rising of the Music of the Flute, at least for one more time, he entered into a meditation at the lap of Kangchendzonga, one of the Himalayan peaks.

But horrible reveries and nightmares haunted him day in and day out and disturbed his concentration. What dreadful sin had he committed that even the meditation was inaccessible for him?

When the world, that he had thrown away somewhere in the course of his journey, was twining around his body, the curtain rose up before him for some new Canto of Kirata, the Reign of Terror.

Everyday he carved and pecked on the stones the nightmares, dreams and reveries that had danced like the angry Lord Siva, the god of destruction, in his brain.

He was acquiring comfort and consolation, without being aware of them, while clapping his hands and laughing aloud like the legendary cynic Bedlam Narayanathu, as those stones were pushed and rolled down to the valley one by one.

Even though the snowstorm was blowing violently outside, his heart was turning hot inside. Slow and steady punitive husk-fire was burning inside his skull!

His eyes were hooked on the sharp teats of Goddess Earth that constantly tickled at the chest of the Sky-god. While staring at the transparency of the silken cloud that tried to cover the nakedness of the Goddess in vain, he tried to know about himself, his very entity.

Who am I? From where did I come to this place? What is the purpose of my life?

If I am born here, I have a right to live here! I am not supposed to roam like a nomad, like a gypsy! Is wandering like a restless-ghost my aim in life? Then, I had done some great sin! If I had committed some great sin, it was only that I had escaped for self-defense, leaving my own mother in the hands of those lecherous barbarians. And if I had escaped like that, I should have to wander until sufficient penance is done!

He drenched with perspiration even in that freezing wind that came to him caressing the virgin snow-clothed Kangchendzonga. His breathing became fast. The life-blood rushed and flowed through his veins. His mind was fully engaged in the effort of discovering himself!

Somewhere I had lost my real name as well as my

genuine identity. Here, I even doubt my own entity. But where had I lost myself…? Oh, where…?

And until I completely performed the penance for the dreadful sin that I had committed, my name would remain to be 'Wanderer'. Simply, the Wanderer…!

Where did I miss my real identity? Did it happen at Erewhon? Erewhon…? Yes, it was there at Erewhon…!

The mountain-slope where, being guided by destiny, he had come for undergoing meditation, aroused in him the powerful memories of the past.

The more he was trying to dissolve himself into the beauty of that Himalayan valley, the more he was undergoing a metamorphosis. He did not feel that it was a disguise or a mask at all, when he turned and transformed himself into a visitor to Erewhon, a name which he had read sometime in the past.

Erewhon? Yes, the country named Erewhon, with all its shocking memories, rolled on before him.

Is it not somewhere there that I had lost myself? But where was that? Oh, where…?

Had I not lost my self somewhere in the darkness of those forts and fortresses which were ruled by the most cruel kings and queens and generals? Had not my individuality disintegrated in the ceaseless tears and endless mourning-sighs of those poor, ignorant and oppressed Erewhonians?

Today, my self is only a mere wanderer! A mere wanderer who, riding in the palanquin of nightmares, tries to color the shadows that appear on the screen of my memory!

The Wanderer stared at a piece of diamond-shaped granite.

He saw in it the figure of his dearest mother country, Erewhon.

> Erewhon! Is she not my homeland? Or...who could ever say of a country that it was his own mother country? Each one of us, being least bothered about anyone else, comes to some part of this world at the odd moments of some morning. Later, we think that that part of the world is our mother country! In fact, what other relationship is there between a person and his country except that of the right of possession? If it is so, my trespassing into Erewhon itself proves and establishes my right over that country. Then simultaneously, Erewhon becomes my mother country and my self turns to be a foreigner there!

The Wanderer started scribbling on that granite with the chisel which was made in the fiery kiln of his heart. The stone was gradually covered with the characters and pictures of those past facts, which were awakened in him, from time to time, through reveries, dreams and nightmares.

> Doesn't this mountain-slope in the lap of Kang-chendzonga and that mountain-slope which bordered Erewhon, look similar? Or are they not one and the same mountain-ranges?
> My self, who had been destined to live a life in some previous age, being pushed out of the womb of my mother, had fallen on a beautiful mountain-slope like this!

The Wanderer's sharp chisel moved along the granite. He began to scribble the history of the re-established Erewhon.

> 'Thus...thus...

Thus the Wanderer arrived at the beautiful mountain-slope. He stood there for a moment enjoying the charming scenario.

Suddenly frightening sounds, like those heard by Butler's protagonist during his first visit, began to rise up from the valley. The first adventurous trip of Butler's hero to Erewhon and his experience during that visit flashed like a lightning through the mind of the Wanderer. He stood there, taking deep breaths as if to empower his mettle for a new life of strenuousness.

> Samuel Butler! Wasn't he a historian? Weren't his writings on Erewhon real historical documents? If so, I know this land and its people. And it turns to be my humble duty to convert these hapless people too! But how...?

He thought for a while how to proselytize and convert the Erewhonians from their traditional religions and foolish creeds. The fact that he was obliged to change their beliefs and convictions made him restless. He slowly walked down to the valley with a determined mind.

Passing the frightful statues which produced horrible sounds when wind blew through their hollow heads, he reached the Mountaineers. They stopped him respectfully and arrested him politely for his criminal trespassing into Erewhon. Surprisingly enough, they kept him under custody simply for the crime that he had no computer in hand!

He stayed in the prison awaiting further orders from the capital. During that time, even the then gaoler's granddaughter began to hate him as he was suffering from an unexpected common cold. Fortunately, before getting any serious disease banned by the country's law, he was ordered to be brought to the capital.

Once he was in the capital of Erewhon, the Protector of Law allowed him to go anywhere he liked. A golden handcuff common in More's Utopia, was given to him, and he walked along the street proudly bearing it as if it were an exclusive ornament of a decoration for his manliness. Strangely enough, criminals were given free passage in the country and the people of Erewhon respected those who wore golden handcuffs. The Wanderer traveled throughout the country, meeting various peoples and witnessing spectacular sights. He observed or rather scrutinized the country like an adventurous journalist and noted down everything in the diary of his brain.

Kingship and imperialism had already ended in Erewhon. When democracy was established, Mister Nosnibor had been sworn in and ruled the country as its president. His reign had been regarded in history as the golden age of Erewhon. The Wanderer came to know that this First President of Erewhon had implemented various rules and regulations as well as many constitutional and administrative reforms for the progress of the country.

These were all mere stories of the far away and the long ago. It was after the second visit of Butler's hero to the capital city that Mister Nosnibor, the pillar of Erewhon or the Erewhonian Diamond, died. The Wanderer remembered for a moment what he had read in Butler's skit about the love and affection shown to the hero by Mister Nosnibor who had recovered to normalcy after a severe, professional treatment for his embezzlement.

After the untimely death of Mister Nosnibor, his daughter was sworn in as the new President of Erewhon and was holding the reins of the administrative machinery. On reaching the capital city, the Wanderer was invited to the palace due to the usual sympathy of the ruling family towards criminals. Chewing the cuds of the sad memory of her father, Mistress Nosnibor said to the Wanderer, "Poor Papa! He could betray the whole people of Erewhon only just before his death. It was because of that sympathy, the whole people of this country had participated in his funeral ceremony!"

There was utter chaos and confusion everywhere in the country just after the demise of Mister Nosnibor. During that uneasy interregnum, there was no one to lead the country and the question raised was, "After Nosnibor, who?" And that is why the people selected Mistress Nosnibor as their new leader, considering her unnatural marriage as well as her great embezzlement in which a bigger amount than in her father's case was involved.

The people loved and respected her because of the sole reason that she had never suffered even from a common cold. Thus, the Wanderer realized that Erewhon was re-established only after an interim administrative break!

The reign of Mistress Nosnibor was remarkable for many reasons. During her time, many Erewhonians were hanged to death for getting banned diseases such as malaria and smallpox. She persecuted all the patients who came to the hospital more than twice, applying the very cruel methods of the police and the soldiers.

However, she honored all the officers who cleverly handled bribery and malfeasance, all the merchants engaged in hoarding and black marketing as well as all the politicians who nurtured nepotism and favoritism, giving them gold medals, silver trophies and certificates on bronze plates. Tears streamed down from her eyes whenever she saw thieves, dacoits, rapists and prostitutes! She was even successful in transforming the disciplined police force into a gang of uniformed criminals, rapists, thieves, sadists and murderers!

The Wanderer also noticed an exclusive change that occurred in Erewhon. He remembered how the Erewhonians who hated all mechanization, had once punished Butler's hero for just using a watch. But, according to the new law, everybody was asked to have computers and televisions, and those who used small machines like watches and transistors were punished mercilessly! The latest rule was that all Erewhonians should use a special computer that tendered full data of all world affairs. Thus, the small farmers who used ploughs to till the land and the small merchants who used bullock-carts to transport farm products were brought under severe punishment.

The Wanderer's hand itched to tear away the mask of the ruler who was imposing computers on the poor people, who turned to prostitution for having no clothes to wear during the daytime and who committed thefts for having no shelter to sleep during the nighttime and who, in the passage of time, slowly succumbed to death by starvation.

The system of Musical Banking in Erewhon was improved considerably. The Musical Bank authorities had succeeded in opening ten to twenty branches even in very small areas. The citizens considered these Musical Banks as an easy way to establish social relationships without causing much financial commitments. There was severe competition among the Musical Banks of different language groups in the opening of branches as well as in the making of the loudest noise. It was a pity that there was not even a single person to extend a helping hand towards those poor Erewhonians who were crushed and strangled under the pressure of such competitions!

To say about the Commercial Banks, most of them operated during the nighttime. Under the cover of darkness, they exchanged currencies and also colored the black money with the white paint. The Government had no objection in depositing the black coins of the Commercial Banks in the Musical Banks. Even Mistress Nosnibor had once received the award introduced by the Government for the best collectors of black coins!

No extraordinary change had come to the system of education in Erewhon. Institutions like the College of Unreason taught only the traditional subjects. The irrational works of such institutions grew more powerful day by day. The University authorities always felt proud of introducing a new system of giving Degrees to all those who offered a huge sum of money. A new barter system of giving Degrees in exchange of capon and coconuts also flourished, especially in the southern parts of Erewhon!

The Government's order was to continue the time-old rotten method of language teaching throughout the country. One of the most important duties of the College of Unreason was to impose a Hypothetical Language named Blah-blah on the majority of the people who did not know it, because it was declared to be the national tongue of Erewhon as it happened to be the mother tongue of almost all the ministers and administrators. Moreover, for the dissemination of news, the Media was using a strange language which was believed to be dead but sparingly used in certain mysterious rites of the Musical Banks.

The Government had generally accepted all the healthy men and women as the most important export commodities of Erewhon. Upon reaching foreign countries, these men and women were delivering great service as slaves and concubines, respectively. The money received for them was utilized solely for the development of the country.

In order to increase the export of this special commodity which earned much foreign exchange, the government had taken great interest in establishing black streets and red streets through out the country. Red clothes were distributed among all the beautiful, young women of the country at a subsidized rate. The Government's Textile Department which had been facing a severe financial crisis due to this special supply completely stopped even the distribution of loincloths for the old and the children.

As the condition of food supply was in the doldrums, the government had encouraged all those who were engaged in political or religious fasting. Moreover, the Musical Banks usually declared fasting-weeks and fasting-months for their customers. The government had issued an order declaring 'Eating till the stomach is full' was not only illegal but also a treason entitled to capital punishment! Moreover, all the beautiful walls of bus-stands and railway stations were covered with notifications like 'Eating is injurious to health' and 'Fast Today, Eat Tomorrow.'

Criminals were given many privileges in Erewhon and the Wanderer enjoyed them to the maximum. He roamed along the streets, witnessing various oddities of the country, which he bore in his mind. But by that time, he faced the attack of malaria, the national taboo! The Supreme Court of Erewhon summoned him for a hearing. Though it had tried the Wanderer for the crimes of trespassing into Erewhon and of having no computer with him, surprisingly enough, it sentenced him to be hanged till death for certain other serious crimes like 'Suffering from a disease, especially malaria,' 'Wearing more than the loincloth' and 'Eating till the stomach is full!'

The Wanderer walked to and fro like a caged musk-cat, in

the darkness of the prison cell. He, being hooked up in the cobweb of cruelty, was quite unwilling to die in a dark cellar, unknown to the outside world. He was not ready to meet death at the hands of those barbarians who blindly believed in the futility of the lives of others. His body, mind and soul were alert in finding out a way to escape.

The gratings of the rusted iron gates of the old chatelet, which were opened and shut in every minute, frightened him. Yet, a glimpse of hope was reaching him through a streak of light that came through a vent hole of the prison cell.

"And thus, the sound and the light seemed to be competing in marring the concentration of the Wanderer…"

The Wanderer stopped his pecking for a while. He became quite restless as the light and the sound were competing even in that valley of Kangchendzonga to disturb his meditation.

The black birds of clouds that brooded over the heaven-touched peaks of the Himalayas beat their wings. The lightning and thunder were flashing and echoing in the valley.

The Wanderer rolled down the first stone on which he had carved the history of the re-established Erewhon, from the terrace of the hill where he was meditating. Would that stone have injured the little finger of Goddess Ganges, down there at the nadir of the valley?

Suddenly, the light and the sound stopped abruptly. The Wanderer's lips began to tremble, after a moment of silence. He chanted the transformed lines from Wordsworth's sonnet:

Butler! Thou shouldst be living at this hour: Erewhon hath need of thee....

The Wanderer was quite mistaken in thinking that the re--established Erewhon would go away from him together with the stone that rolled down the valley.

'Erewhon is immortal! She cannot be erased either from history or from his mind!'

She haunted him like a ghost and hunted him like a nightmare.

'Erewhon is my mother, is part and parcel of my soul.'

But, he never thought that such a sacred relationship would turn into an abhorred chain!

A heavy chain or rather a slavish yoke on my neck...! Was I not a mere bullock destined to bear the yoke of memory and pull the plough...?

But, am I alone...? Don't you know that the majority of Erewhonians live just like animals? If so, my own history itself is the history of an average Erewhonian!

The poor Erewhonian! He was fated to live a life solely to wander and labor! The plodders of Time! The poor bullocks which were turning the sugar-mill, keeping their heads under the heavy yokes of life! And that is what an Erewhonian is!

The Wanderer sharpened his chisel and started carving the history on another stone. The annals of the helpless bullocks that worked hard day in and day out for the pleasure of others!

'Rather an autobiography…!'

That's it! Of the poor, emasculated bullocks of Erewhon…!

Once upon a time, I was a bull - healthy, wealthy and wise. But today I am a mere bullock and I do not know who made me a bullock. I do not even remember who had castrated me. My owner? Or myself? I do not know exactly. And as a Bullock I will never know!

My owner who rules me has placed a heavy yoke on my neck so that I cannot but look downwards. I am pulling the big yoke with the great expectations of getting my daily bread, water and shelter. And where ignorance is bliss, it is folly to be wise and, thus, for me food becomes the be all and end all.

I do not know where I am going. I know only one thing that I am working, working and working. And I always look downwards due to the heavy weight of my yoke so that I can see only a few paces ahead of me.

I am walking, walking and walking without rest. My owner tells me repeatedly that I am walking forward, towards progress. And he further quotes the distorted lines of Robert Frost, 'Miles to go before you sleep, and miles to go before you sleep.' Even all the predecessors of my present controller conveniently kept this slogan always in their pockets.

With the passing of time, my tired legs are covering miles and miles. I continue my walk without stop and work hard without getting food or rest. And I am sure that my owner has tied one end of my yoke to the rotating wooden turnstile of a machine that squeezes sugarcanes. Now and then, he goes to the press and quenches his thirst by drinking the sugarcane juice which is the product of my blood and sweat. While I die of thirst with sweat and heat…and my body undergoes weathering, alas!

My owner usually preaches in my ears, 'Late to bed and early to rise make a bullock healthy, wealthy and wise.' And I am always sincere in my work and obedient to my owner. Moreover, he always assures me that castration makes a bull more healthy and vigorous. He had promised me food, shelter and protection when I surrendered myself for the emasculation. But I am sure that as a bullock I will ever remain weak, poor and ignorant.

I do not know my owner's future plans for me. I am walking and walking, working and working. How long have I to walk? What is my destiny and which is my destination? I am walking along the same road which I had passed years ago! As I tread the beaten track with a new environment, I sense only the rotten smell of my own blood and sweat!

I walk and work, wondering over the weird names of my owner and of his damned sugar mill. I sigh and cry, absorbing the lilt and tone of the optimistic farmer who sings, *'If winter comes, can spring be far behind?'*

The Wanderer laughed aloud as another stone of history too rolled down towards the dale. At the end of that meaningless laugh, he sighed, cursing his own little frailties.

Who are these bullocks? The fact that I am not alone or other bullocks are with me will not reduce my grief.

Sorrow will never cease, even though we generalize it! And the pity is that we are all mere bullocks, plodding day in and day out without knowing our sad plight! Those who are always destined to pull the cart laden heavily with the burden of their lives!

Again, a problem cannot be solved simply by the display of it. Perhaps, we are all the mere waste of the sugarcane! The waste of sugarcane that once oozed out its lifeblood to sweeten the lives of others!

Or else, we may be those fowls that try to live on feeding the worms and vermin among the waste of the sugarcane thrown away by someone after enjoying its sweet juice! But, even then, are there not team-fights among the fowls that were seeking food with a single aim, based on a unanimously accepted principle? Don't we see around us the hens, the so-called exalted mother-image, that peck at and chase away their chickens when they eagerly approach the food they found by mere chance?

The Wanderer despairingly remembered that he too was fallen among that brood of chickens who did not know how to live.

But, when one tries to acquire knowledge with an irresistible thirst of freedom, slavish chains fall around one's neck!

The Wanderer wondered at the meaninglessness of getting citizenship even for bullocks, donkeys, dogs and fowls in Erewhon where one did not enjoy even the right to live.

The pathetic picture of the poor chicken, drawn from the Malayalam saying, that were trying to deaden their hunger among the wastes of the sugarcane, really agonized him. He selected a new stone and began to peck the history of a hen and her chickens on it...

**B**reaking the chains of bondage, one by one, the chickens crashed their eggshells and came out from the darkness of ignorance into the daylight of freedom. For the realization of the hopes and ambitions piled up in their hearts, they looked up at the face of the Mother Hen who stood before them, holding up her head with the arrogance of a true protector.

The Mother Hen had never thought that the hatching of those eggs which she had been using as mere pawns of her purely selfish-relaxation, though most of them were not even laid by her, would create such difficulties and obligations for her. But, by then, she had realized that it was clever on her part to allow those byproducts of her indolence to grow up as it would help to establish her supremacy over other fowls.

In a few days, the chickens that began to taste the narcotic effect of freedom in the hallucinations of light became quite aware of their birthright. They became restless, when they learned the truth that the Mother Hen, who always tried to suppress them and keep them under her wings, was not at all interested in rendering the universally recognized duty of a true mother.

The poor chicks foolishly hoped that their mother would also give them milk from her breasts like the mothers of those rabbits, lambs and calves who were living happily around them. Day by day, the feeling that the drinking of milk from one's mother's breasts is simply a birthright grew stronger and stronger in them.

One day, after many days of roosting, they ran around their mother playfully and said in a lisping voice, "Mother Hen! If you are our true mother, please give us your nipples to suck, like all other mothers."

The unexpected demand from the chickens shocked the Mother Hen for a moment. After a few minutes of brooding, she retained the balance of her mind and began to think very seriously over the issue.

The Mother Hen understood that it was because of their legs that the chickens ran around her and made such complaints. So, she said with an air of assurance, "Lo! My dear chicks! Look around you! Those young ones who drink their mother's milk have got four legs! And only those creatures either having four legs or without legs are getting milk from their mother's breasts. Therefore, if you insist on drinking milk from my udder, come to me after cutting away your legs. Then I shall give you milk directly from my nipples."

The chickens returned happily and pecked at each other's legs and broke them away. The next day, the legless chicks flew around their mother and said, "Mother Hen! See, we've cut off our legs! Now, give us milk from your breasts."

The Mother Hen knew that it was because of their wings that the chickens flew around her and irritated her with their complaints. So, she said with an air of certainty, "My darlings! Watch carefully those young ones around you who feed on their mother's milk! None of them has wings! So, my dear chickens, go and cut away your wings and come back, I shall give you milk from my own udder."

The chickens did not lose their hopes! They pecked at each other and broke away their wings. The next day, the chickens, which had lost their legs and wings, rolled around their mother and said, "Mother Hen! Please give milk from your breast to these poor chicks that have neither legs nor wings."

Knowing that the chickens, even though they had lost their legs with which they had been walking on land as well as the wings with which they had been fluttering in the air, were still pressing their claim, the Mother Hen cackled aloud and said with a laugh, "As far as you have neither legs nor wings, you'll soon get milk from my breast, if only you could just fulfill one more condition. Go away now, and come back after removing your backbones. You can *see* my teats then coming out."

Though the chickens knew that it was their backbones that helped them to roll towards their mother, they pecked at each other and broke away their backbones, just for the sake of asserting their birthright of getting their mother's milk. At times, even the Mother Hen, out of her kindness, helped them in breaking the strong backbones of some of the chickens.

The next day, the chickens, being incapable of moving their bodies, lay paralyzed and shouted, "Mother Hen, give us your milk at least now! Please, have mercy on us who are bereft of our legs, wings and backbones."

The voice of the chickens resounded all over the country. Their sighs and sobs echoed from pole to pole, from horizon to horizon. Their wail of woe broke the hearts of other creatures whose young ones were feeding on the milk of their mothers. Rabbits, lambs and calves stood silent and motionless.

When the voice of the chickens became unbearable to the Mother Hen, she grumbled, "The voice of these fools will ever be a nuisance to me. How can I give my own milk to these chickens without undergoing a fundamental change of my body? Therefore, if I stop their sound too, I can continue my dominance without any more complaints from them."

The Mother Hen went towards the chickens and talked to them with an air of sympathy and reconciliation, 'My dearest chicks! Don't you know what a great sacrifice I am doing simply by ruling you? Look around you and watch those creatures that suck the nipples of their mothers! None of them had beaks but mere lips to suck at their Mothers' breasts. Therefore, if you pull away your beaks, I shall give you milk from my own udder. And see, my teats are coming out."

The desperate and helpless chickens, having no other choice or alternative means, began to peck each other and pull away their beaks, lying wherever they were!

In that attempt, some of the chickens lost their tongues and some others their eyes! Some of them even lost their heads. While watching that horrible, heartbreaking spectacle, the Mother Hen cackled aloud with concealed joy and delight. And it was all merely fun for her!

Fortunately, a sudden enlightenment came among a few of the chickens, who were lying completely exhausted of that reciprocal fight. They immediately ceased their mutual attack and began to brood over the matter.

Within no time, they realized the truth that they could not drink milk from the breast of their mother as they were deprived of their beaks! They also understood that the Mother Hen, on whom they had faithfully depended all these years, would never undergo any fundamental change, and that they should seek some other means to gain and establish their birthright.

They resolved adamantly to take revenge on the Mother Hen who had been cheating them all these days with splendid promises, as well as to concentrate their power in getting actual recognition for their birthright.

They waited for that heaven-sent moment of the best opportunity, with the hope that Time would enable them in regaining their lost legs and wings; their beaks and backbones! They waited and waited silently and patiently…

The cry of the feeble and fragile chickens that were waiting patiently for their birthright resounded in the ears of the Wanderer. Ugh! A land of arrogant hens that dole out promises, impossible to perform! But...

Is this really the sound of those weaklings?

The Wanderer looked around. The sun had gone away and was hiding somewhere beyond the horizon. The valley was dozing in the evening twilight that reflected from the snow-gown of Kangchendzonga.

Am I not hearing the chattering of the birds which were flying here and there to roost on the branches of the Banyan Tree that gave me shade during the daytime? Ah! The immortal Tree!

Where are those chickens and the Mother Hen? Yes! Now they live only on the stone that I just chiseled. Let this stone roll down, down to the base of the valley! Let it roll and roll, and down there, take refuge in the safe hands of Goddess Ganges!

The quarrel of the roosting birds ended. They, hiding behind the twigs and leaves of the everlasting Banyan Tree, began to see dreams. Yet, their voice resounded in the ears of the Wanderer like the humming of some musical instrument.

A humming that pierces the thickness of the darkness! The humming of the mosquitoes which grow and multiply in the warmth that is left sometimes by the sun during the day! The mosquitoes that are intoxicated by drinking on the paucity of sweetness that is left out still in the waste of sugarcanes!

The humming of the mosquitoes hunted him as he was sitting quite exhausted, on his sack-couch. The bedbugs that came out quietly from the cracks of the couch brushed at his legs with their feelers.

"I know about their aim!" the Wanderer murmured restlessly. "My blood, that's what they want! My lifeblood which is my being and everything…!"

The Wanderer wondered at the nuance of behavior between mosquitoes and bedbugs, though they have the one and the same aim.

On one side the bedbugs who labor silently for my blood, and on the other, the mosquitoes who cry aloud for my blood! And my blood is the sole aim of both the groups!!

Both sides may have got their own points of argument. And both groups may have their own principles. Both groups could become successful even in proving those principles reasonably, and getting them recognized by the masses.

The Wanderer looked helplessly at the Goddess of Sleep who slipped away from him. With a heavy sigh, he began to think deeply, patiently bearing that trauma and painful loneliness!

The most important things are evidences and their interpretations! Evidences are inevitable to prove a theory, however ridiculous it is! Proverbs, precedence, traditional habits, ancient unwritten laws, modern written laws and what not are all evidences! However, the importance of the matter mainly depends on the method of interpretation with which one should prove the theory.

"Somewhere I had noted it down! But where was it? Where…?

Keeping his chisel in his right hand and caressing his bearded cheeks with his left hand, the Wanderer tried to recollect his past days. He took an old diary and slowly turned its pages one by one. He stared at the last paragraph on the last page of that diary and whispered, "Sleep is essential even at the cost of blood."

Where was I when I scribbled this line? Was it not written when I was spending my days in the dark prison-cell of Erewhon? Had I not jotted down these insincere words then to find out a temporary justification for my own fear and incapability which I suffered at the zenith of my languor?

The Wanderer apprehended that the bedbugs which crawled under him and the mosquitoes that flew around him were bringing new dimensions of meaning to that sentence in his diary.

Any absurd theory can be enforced upon and be accepted by a society that has lost its retaliatory powers as well as its natural reflective tendency, simply by displaying certain major evidences! Yes! They should be displayed! These epics of mosquitoes and bedbugs are, perhaps, helpful at least for those who wish to take Doctorate Degrees by doing research in the field of Sociology or Political Science.

He burnished his chisel and began to peck on a small piece of granite. Those points of arguments displayed by the bloodthirsty mosquitoes and bedbugs for the universal acceptance of their selfish motives! They too should become part and parcel of history! A lesson for the seekers of Truth! He scribbled hurriedly on the stone with his sharp chisel…

A clear truth that can be derived from the book, 'Origin of Species,' written by a white man: According to the Theory of Evolution, Man is evolved from Mosquito.

An Anthropologist has written thus in his diary: Mosquitoes might have been born either at the freezing temperature of Tibet or at the scorching temperature of the Dark Continent or at the temperate climate of Middle Asia.

Another Anthropologist also emphasized: Bedbugs also came into existence more or less at the same period itself together with mosquitoes.

A Sociologist has scribbled like this: The social life of mosquitoes is a highly complex one. From the Pre-historic Period onwards, Mosquitoes have an unbreakable relation-ship with human beings. The truth is that today the mosquito has become a global phenomenon.

An immortal Historian has written thus in golden letters: From time to time, Mosquitoes have been trying to achieve power through world wars and civil wars. Thus, the demonstration of power by the yellow mosquitoes on the brown mosquitoes and the attempt of the white mosquitoes to establish their supremacy over the black mosquitoes are events of great significance.

From the diary of an Optimist: It is quite a consolation that Mosquitoes, realizing that the wars and the rebellions would lead towards the extinction of their own species from this planet, gave shape to an international organization which is pledged to end wars forever.

But a Pessimist made a note like this: There is no doubt that the global organization erected by the mosquitoes to re-establish peace will crumble down to pieces. The truth is that the blood thirst, which is the basic reason for all wars, will undoubtedly dig the grave of this organization too!

Adam, the First Mosquito, said like this: What is there in the loss of Paradise? How blissful it is to get at least the forbidden fruit!

The truth that is revealed through Matsya Nyaya in Artha Sastra, written by a brahmin named Chanakya: It is inevitable for existence that big mosquitoes must swallow small mosquitoes. Even fish that live in water also do the same!

An underlined sentence in the manifesto of Mosquitoes reads thus: Our aim is to lull humanity with a humming. But, for that they should have to give us just a bit of their blood.

From the personal diary of President Manu who codified laws

for the first time: The aim of Mosquitoes is not merely to put human beings to sleep by singing a lullaby. The scheme of carrying these sleeping human beings away is also included in our Five Year Plans.

What is emphasized in the Laws of Chairman Moses who led his people from Egypt to Palestine: Human beings have realized, though a bit late, the truth that mosquitoes would peck them away. They have started to nurture bedbugs! And the Balance of Power has turned to be the landmark of the Modern Age.

However in the manifesto of Bedbugs, it is said like this: We bite the human beings and keep them close to their beds lest the mosquitoes should carry them away in the loneliness of the night. In return for this service, the human beings have to give us a bit of their blood.

The following are the points of argument chalked out and raised during the First Round Table Conference of the International Organization shaped by the Mosquitoes:

The Bedbug: Blood is the very entity of life. The color of blood is red. Therefore, our color also is red. Yet our final goal is white color. And we drink the blood of human beings just for the existence of our species.

The Mosquito: Our permanent color is black. But we change our color in accordance with the environment. Green, Blue or White, are all one and the same to us. Drinking human blood is not a common habit of our species. However, members of our fair-sex drink human blood. And, as the female is inevitable for the multiplication of our species, we even accept the color red to a certain extent.

From the Peace Treaty, signed simultaneously by both the leaders of Mosquitoes and Bedbugs: Whatever is the color of flags and banners, we must stick to our own aims and duties. For the realization of our common end to prolong the existence of our species, we must co-operate in drinking the blood of human beings, the so-called rational animals, who really sleep and who sometimes feign themselves to be asleep.

The size of the granite was too small! Would this ill-mannered ending create bewilderment among the Seekers of Truth?

The Wanderer was all confused. He desperately threw away the stone, the whole surface of which was completely carved, down into the valley. Then he returned to his sack-couch, opened his diary and read the last page of it, once again:

"Sleep is essential even at the cost of blood."
Is it really the theory that I nurtured during my days in Erewhon? If so, I am a fool, an idiot, a manifestation of utter indolence!
He read aloud, in its full form, the last page of his dog-eared diary:
"Hail Mosquito, praise be to thee, for you lull me to sleep! Hail Bedbug, glory be to thee, for you keep me close

to the couch! Sleep is essential even at the cost of blood! And so, to whoever had discovered the Balance of Power Theory, Alleluia! Alleluia!!"

From the fingers which were tired of stone-carving, his diary slipped down to the floor. The Wanderer felt himself deprived of strength and he too collapsed on his sack-couch. Then his heart was throbbing heavily and he felt them like the drum beats of some jungle folks.

Here, in this holy valley of the Himalayas, there is no place for the blood suckers! Here, they have no existence at all. In the extreme cold of this valley, mosquitoes and bedbugs extirpate themselves...

The Wanderer slept, forgetting everything. But, in some odd moments of the night, he was startled out of his sleep, as if he had seen a nightmare. The sound of the rats that played around his couch in great rejoicing and exhilaration frightened him...

Is it solely the sound of mice, rats and bandicoots? Is it not the disgusting voice of all the exploiters that join hands with these gnawing creatures? And moreover, I am not hearing this sound for the first time! Is it not the same sound that had rung in my ears while staying in the prison-cell of Erewhon? Is it not the same noise that I have just heard in the nightmare while lying in an inert slumber on this sack-couch, in the lap of Kangchendzonga?

The Wanderer tried to recollect that nightmare through which a poor farmer of Erewhon had revealed to him the painful story of his life. A tragedy that would be faced by all

Erewhonian farmers at some time in their lives! The Wanderer hurriedly took his chisel and began to peck on another piece of granite. His lips trembled and his heart palpitated.

> This too must become a part of history. Yes! The cruelty of the exploiters who unite themselves with idealistic mottoes and enthusiastic slogans to make the lives of the poor cassava-cultivators of Erewhon, miserable and unbearable!

The Wanderer once again saw with his mind's eye the visage of that Erewhonian who had appeared in his nightmare. He started striking at the stone with re-doubled force and spirit, as his hammer fell again and again on the top of the chisel... carving lines and figures on the hard granite...

It was not from the pompous orations of the politicians that we, the ordinary farmers, learned about exploitation and the exploiters. For, we, the illiterate mass, could not understand most of the flowery terminology and puzzling statistics presented to us through the election pamphlets and manifestos of the political parties!

In fact, it was our own experience that taught us all about exploitations to which we were doomed. For instance, we the farmers who cultivated cassava for earning our daily bread learned from our own constant experience, that it was the rats and the birds who exploited us for ages!

Now, about the rats, taking their grotesque shapes and

horrible behavior into consideration, we had already declared unanimously that they by nature were exploiters. Every night they prowled into our cassava-farms and destroyed our dear plants in the solitude of midnight, as if always sticking to their motto, 'A cassava plant, a night.'

Now, please do not think of us as mere fools or impotent people. Let us frankly admit that in bygone days we had to take weapons in our hands against these veteran exploiters. And see, these cruel exploiters usually mistook our tolerance for cowardice!

No wonder that this class of veteran exploiters, who always emphasized the sanctity of the slogan, 'Unity is Power', sought the friendship and co-operation of other similar classes of exploiters. And such unholy alliances were natural as we too believed in the principle of 'Concordia discord'.

But we were really shocked when we realized that the class of birds who always lived together with us as our intimate friends, who always helped to keep our health in tact by offering us meat and eggs and who even always poured vitality into our tired minds through their wonderful songs, had made treaty with the perennial exploiting class of the rats.

Thence forward, the rats that crawled into our farms during the nights, rejected their old slogan, 'A cassava plant, a night,' and left the place after digging about the crown of many plants and eating only bits from every rootstock.

It was only later that we found out the secret of their new technique. It actually benefited the birds like the fowls and the crows that visited our farms during the day time. They completely consumed the rest of the cassava-roots, fully peeled but left unfinished during the night by the rats.

See! How the great word 'unity' which was exalted by our sages of yesteryears had become here the byword of these exploiters of poor farmers!

Moreover, we were really perplexed when these exploiting classes very successfully practiced the principles of reciprocal help and co-operation which were always revered but deemed impracticable by the farmers.

This, of course, needed further illustration. We, the farmers, usually fixed nets to trap the birds that came to destroy our harvest. But the rats that entered our farms in the silence of the night gnawed at all such nets and thus saved their co-exploiters from danger!

Now, just think! The organized labor of these exploiting classes! Isn't their organized labor worthy of emulation? Yes! Just think of that!!

Surprisingly enough, these exploiting classes were far ahead of us in mutual love and selfless sacrifice too! In this matter, the fowls exceeded all other creatures and, thanks to Darwinian Theory of Evolution, it was the fowls that offered a link to the species of rats that walked on the ground and the species of birds that flew in the sky. When we placed poisonous food in and around our farms to kill the rats, these fowls that came out in the daytime, pecked and swallowed every part of it!

How pathetic is our plight! At times, we even feel that the very word 'forlorn' haunts us all through our life! What a sad and helpless situation we are in! We simply distort our mouth with a cynical smile! Alas! Alas!

What else could we, the farmers, do when our favorite fowls that had given us eggs and meat, died of rat-poison, but simply weep over their untimely death?

As long as these exploiting classes were not at all reluctant to practice literally the great Christian principle, 'There is no greater love than sacrificing one's life for another,' what else could we do but bear the burden of life tolerating their constant atrocities?

Or, what other means of struggle could we adopt, expecting a beneficial end, against these exploiting classes than that well-tried principle, 'Take Weapon in Hands?'

And think, if we were too feeble before the rats and the birds, how could we proceed with our struggles against the dealers in cassava roots and the manufacturers of tapioca?

Down with the rats! Down with the birds! Down with their squeaks and crows! If the uproar and shouts of a people could bring down the wall of Jericho, our slogans that resound in the street and our fists in the air signifying vengeance will break this citadel too!

**W**hen one dream gradually vanishes, another one suddenly appears at nobody's beck and call! Where has gone the pain-stricken face of that Erewhonian cassava-cultivator?

His firm voice still resounded in the ears of the Wanderer...

*'Against these exploiting classes, take weapon in hands... take weapon in hands... take weapon...'*

But... the culture of love and patience, dissolved in the very blood itself and deep-rooted in the pith and marrow of life, numbs the hands. And then, dangerous weapons slip down from them...

How could a people, rich only in their culture and tradition, organize an armed revolt against this silent exploitation? What law or justice could be pointed out to chain the murderous white-cat, in a country where the doves were killed and were ignorant of one another's fate?

Am I not also included in the group of those who try to believe blindly that the extinction of the dove-species will not occur, even though they are killed one by one, just in front of our eyes? Are we not among the people who simply scratch at the stinking sores of their noses, being incapable of distinguishing the stench disseminated by the rotten carcasses of doves, the martyrs in genocides? Perhaps the reign of an arrogant ruler or a wicked Prime Minister who puts the cat among the pigeons may be inevitable...

The Wanderer's body shivered head to foot. 'No! No! The doves are immortal beings! Death is not for them!' His mind whispered. His hands itched. And he pecked on the stone with a renewed spirit and vitality... the annals of the poor doves...

Then... It was the age of the sovereign power! The era of the epoch-making kings and emperors...! The good old time of the best benevolent despots...! And the glorious days of the doves...!

The peace-loving, great king ruled the kingdom without any personal worries or public problems. Just like the reign of Mahabali, the legendary Asura king of Kerala in the folksong:

'When Maveli ruled this country,
All human beings had equal status,

And there was no theft, cheating or lies,
No fake balance, measures or weights...'

The Prime Minister, who had represented the people, helped the king in all administrative matters. And the doves flew wherever they liked...

The subjects spent their graceful days in true happiness. No one had ever heard of starvation-deaths. Nowhere in the country, were there racial hatred or caste differences, nor was there the supremacy of the priests.

The doves raised their humming-chirp everywhere in the country. They hopped about the palace, the throne and the flagstaff. They built their nests on the roof of the palace. Having nothing to fear, they walked and hopped and flew around in complete ignorance of the sense of fear. And the bell-beat of their wings resounded all over the country.

However, the king or his subjects or even the doves did not know at first that the Prime Minister, who was the people's representative, had been nurturing and bringing up a white-cat under his roof, just near his foot!

And the white-cat day by day grew fatter and fatter, eating stolen food. It enjoyed all rights and acquired more of them by rubbing its body against the legs of the Prime Minister or tickling him with its raised tail and, at times, even sitting on his lap. That white monster, which ate only vegetarian food, gradually became successful in stealing the lion's share from the food allotted to the subjects and the doves. In fact, the Prime Minister felt proud of such mean and base activities of his favorite white-cat.

As time passed, the horrible voice of the white-cat began to echo in the palace. Later, that voice spread to every nook and corner of the country, polluting the whole atmosphere.

Even then, the king and his subjects failed to distinguish

the horror in the voice of the white-cat. Only the doves, being afraid of the voice, fluttered away from the throne and the flag-staff, and tried to stick around their nests on the roof of the palace.

By then, the curtain fell to the glorious reign of the king. The Prime Minister who was the representative of the people, captured the power, and taking the crown and scepter for himself, he exiled the king. The King's Throne became the Minister's Throne. And the Prime Minister soon proclaimed to the nation, through palace-criers and drum-beaters, that the doves were dangerous to the nation as well as to the native citizens.

But the subjects, who always loved the doves, could not understand the Prime Minister's new language. The truth that the doves still roosted on the roof of the palace consoled them. And they blindly believed that the extinction of the dove-species would never happen.

As days passed, a sort of horrible stench began to come out of the roof of the palace, the name of which was changed into a more democratic rhyming-word, the Minister's Mansion. Only the Prime Minister knew that the white-cat was engaged in killing the doves, roosting and settled on the attic of the palace.

The nauseous stench that at first was hanging only around the palace premises, gradually spread out to the other parts of the country. But the Prime Minister proudly declared that it was the odor coming out of his mouth, and the subjects tried to believe it.

At last, when the nasty smell became unbearable, the white-robed and the red-robed people of the country, one day, rushed to the Minister's Mansion. They caught the Prime Minister by the neck and pushed him out of the palace.

Only then, the Prime Minister and the subjects came to know that there was really a stinking sore inside the swollen nose of the Prime Minister, caused by the constant breathing of the stench that had been coming out of the attic, for many years.

The people who searched the attic of the Minister's Mansion stood paralyzed for a moment, seeing the decomposed carcasses of the doves scattered everywhere under the cupola and over the ceiling. They stood motionless, disbelieving the fact that the doves that were always loved and respected by them, had met with an inevitable, tragic genocide.

In a corner of the attic, the white-cat, which was fattened by eating the flesh of the doves, was still lying asleep. Though its snoring frightened the people, with great indignation they caught it, tied a rope to its tail, hanged it upside down on a pole and displayed it to the passersby.

Later, they swept the attic and the roof and cleansed the palace and threw down the feathers of the dead doves from the terrace of the Minister's Mansion. Then, a great miracle happened as if to give a permanent consolation to the despair stricken multitudes!

Life came to the feathers of the dead doves... to the feathers that were gliding and dancing in the air! Each one of them, like the phoenix bird that flew up out of its own pyre, transformed itself into a dove! They fluttered around the palace, hopped about the throne and the flagstaff, and perched on the roof of the palace! They made their new nests inside the cupola and showered joy and rapture to the subjects by sounding their humming-chirp.

The white-cat, that was still hanging head downwards, writhed and struggled and wailed on the pole to which it had been tied. No wonder that the white-cat, hanging like Vetal, the phantom of the accursed Brahmin-ghost in the Vikramaditya Stories, was still dreaming that the asses called the public would soon feel sympathy towards it and, then it could regain its power and glory, in vain...

The voice of the white-cat comes like a chain of waves even towards this holy lap of Kangchendzonga. What a frightful voice! Are the white-cats immortal, just like the doves? Are they too deathless...? If so... If so...

The Wanderer, being filled with more disgust than despair, threw down the stone on which a part of history was scribbled.

Let the white-cats wail, hanging upside down from the poles! Let those flag-staves be their gibbets! Then only the doves could walk and hop and fly, freely and rampantly.

Let the dethroned kings and the ousted ministers go to the forest and accept the deserted jungle as their sanctum sanctorum. And, let the wailing of the white-cats be drowned in the cooing of the doves!

But... Will that palace, which has been changed into the Minister's Mansion, be deserted? Will that throne, which has been altered into the Minister's Masnud, remain vacant? Will it be ruined by rust and dust? Will spiders spread their nets over it? And...! What will be the future of the country when the spiders, the notorious synonym for cruelty, take up the scepter and crown of the country?

The reign of a she-spider may be an inevitability of history. Is it not the reason why a she-spider with golden cobweb, occupied the throne of Erewhon and settled on it?

The frightful figure of the she-spider crept into the mind of the Wanderer.

The colorful and charming she-spider... and that is only the outward appearance. But, under that serpentine beauty, the strong poison of cruelty is brewing up to the brim...

For a moment, the Wanderer became as quiet as a philosopher.

Yes! The cruelty...! Cruelty... it is inherent in each and every living being. But the earth would have become *without form and void*, if all the living beings had expressed this intrinsicality in its full and pure form. And that is why Nature, with her invisible power, controls cruelty to a certain extent.

For instance, cruelty for the sake of existence is justifiable and allowable. We can take it for granted when one creature kills another as part of its food acquirement. But it is unnatural, rather against the Law of Nature, if creatures fight each other for the prolongation of their power and perpetuation of their glory...

No special introduction is needed when a historian like me reveals this natural truth through a parable, for no one is here, who is not familiar with the traditional way of living followed by the species to which the protagonist of this parable belongs. Everyday we watch and hear about such cruelties as well as Nature's reaction towards them, and so, they too must become a part of history...

The Wanderer took a big piece of black granite and began to peck on it. He chiseled the caption, 'The Tragedy of the

Spidress' and, then, scribbled down the pitiful and fearful history of a she-spider: Once upon a time...

Once upon a time, somewhere lived a spidress. She lived without cares and worries at the centre of a beautiful garden. Various plants and trees of the garden sang lullabies for her and flowers of different colors rocked her to sleep.

But, it would be fairly correct to say that the garden had received and respected her only because of its hospitality, deep rooted in its ancient culture. To be precise, as everybody knew, her ancestors had come from outside the garden, as mere refugees, and had established their right over it through attack, conquest and annexation.

As the garden and its members, from big trees to just trivial plants, began to respect the family of spiders, they themselves became proud and arrogant. No wonder, the heroine of our story also inherited the traditional arrogance of the spider family.

Generally speaking, is it not the tradition of the spider species that they grow up by eating their own mother's body? Is it not also an exclusive habit with them that they kill and eat even their own mates, after sexual intercourse? How can we ignore such facts as mere Indian superstitions? Just imagine how cruel and unnatural their way of living is!

Our heroine too grew up, slowly gnawing at and consuming up the body of her own mother. Her mother could not kill and eat her mate as he was clever enough to slip away after the mating or hide in another part of the garden or seek another female. And that is why, when our spidress grew up and attained maturity, she welcomed her father, and with his help started a new life.

Another reason for the arrogance of our spidress was her exclusive ability to make golden cobwebs. As she became old enough to weave her own cobweb, she made one golden gossamer and, quite accidentally, became aware of her talent. She not only became proud of it but also defamed other spiders and even attacked them and, at times, chased them out of the garden.

Our heroine gradually extended her golden net to all parts of the garden. At times, she encroached even on the neighboring gardens and tried to spread her net over them. Above the garden, her web hung like a golden canopy that glittered in the bright daylight. The trees, plants and bushes foolishly believed that they were quite safe under her golden cobweb. She confirmed, and even guaranteed them that bees, beetles and butterflies from foreign gardens would come to them.

Soon, the spidress began to rule the garden like an autocrat. Bees and beetles and butterflies came to her, being attracted by the magical colors and mesmerizing fragrance of the flowers. But she claimed that it was because of the magnetic power of her golden web. Whatsoever, all of them were trapped in the golden web, and they waited in a state of panic for their death. For, once they were caught into the stickiness of the web, neither could they move their legs nor their wings!

Our heroine had taken a free view of life and an open way of living, both in her private and public life. When she attained maturity, she herself searched out a suitable mate and mated with him according to the Law of Nature.

And then, after sexual intercourse...? As the he-spider was dozing in the exhaustion of mating, the spidress, after an

45

interim surrender before her mate, recollected all her might and gormandized on him rapaciously, as if taking revenge against him who had kept the strength of her body and the power of her mind down for at least a few minutes!

Seeing that cruel spectacle, the plants of the garden fainted; the flowers faded. The big trees stood thunderstruck. Nature, trembling in her wrath, waited for her chance to take revenge!

As the days passed, the weight in her abdomen increased. Though she felt much tired, she was always found engaged in polishing her golden web and repairing it. And when the time approached for the laying of eggs, she made two plates with the substance of her own cobweb. She laid her eggs in one plate, covered them with the other and stitched them together closely and splendidly.

In fact, all the eggs laid by her were too small. She was afraid that if the trees and plants growing under her net came to know that she, who was ruling and controlling that great garden, had laid only tiny eggs, they would laugh at her. And that is why she kept all her miniature eggs in a box and gave it the shape of a large egg. She continued her day-to-day life, keeping that nidus very close to her bosom, as if declaring to the world that she had laid an egg which was as big as her!

At first she had only the self-assertive feeling that the eggs laid by her should be under her legs. But, as days passed the fear that the young ones, once they were hatched out, would wind up her freedom and question her power and authority, gradually grew in her. So, she decided that her young ones should grow only inside the nidus.

As the eggs were hatched, the swarm of little-spiders tried to break the egg-box and come out of it. They began to gnaw at the upper lid of the nidus and became successful in making a hole in it just under the stomach of the spidress. They continued their gnawing and gradually began to carve into the chest of their mother! At first, the spidress had not cared seriously about the matter, as she had been keeping the nidus tightly to her bosom.

Later, even when she was running here and there in pain and with panic, she was not prepared to give freedom to her young ones. She blindly believed that it was better to die a martyr than giving freedom to her spider-kids at the expense of her own power and authority.

As a final attempt for her own survival, she had not hesitated even to bite and murder a young spider that had first succeeded in coming out of the egg-box! But, by then, she was quite exhausted from her plight and she felt the pangs of senility and decrepitude.

We could easily guess the end of this story! Here too, like in all other tragedies, Nemesis, the goddess of Justice, played her usual part, of course, an ordinary routine-work for her!

The spider-kids rapaciously gnawed at the chest, stomach and groin of their own mother. The spidress breathed her last, still gripping at her golden cobweb. The swarm, rejoicing at their independence, threw away their mother's carcass to the ground and established their power and authority over the golden cobweb.

Nature stood awestruck for a moment, silently bearing witness to the repetition of history! Then, she laughed aloud, being quite satisfied with the implementation of justice! The big trees nodded their heads, the plants smiled furtively and bushes swayed jovially. The flowers sighed in relief and smiled in their natural gaiety...

**B**ig trees shake their heads and little plants dance in the chill breeze that blows from Kangchendzonga. Can the chill breeze incite fragrance, hues and vitality in flowers?

The Wanderer noticed the ants crowding on the ground under him. They were dragging the dead body of some she-spider. They were pulling and pushing at the carcass and were dragging it wherever they pleased. They were running here and there, independently, as if indiscipline is their freedom!

But… How long can they prolong their joy and rapture? Is there any legal control for their free movements? And, is not freedom without discipline mere anarchy? Or… why should we simply blame the ants? Each one of us gives our own definitions to freedom, and one's definition differs from another's! Have I not realized this truth, when I heard the experience of an Erewhonian Merchant, while roaming through the streets of Erewhon? What a pathetic story…! A story narrated from his heart of hearts! The story of Nausea or Inko!

The Wanderer remembered each and every word of that Erewhonian Merchant. He selected a new piece of granite from the mountain slope.

How could I forget such a narration of one's firsthand experience, a fact stranger than fiction? And it must come to light in his own words and it must be carved on a new piece of stone. Let those who study history get delight out of it and think deeply over it... over the various definitions of freedom...! How each one reacts to freedom and how a particular definition misleads an individual...!

It was quite unexpectedly that we met Nausea, in that Month of August, and became acquainted with him. As our country was celebrating a Grand Carnival, the city was filled with stampedes and crowds.

And the city, just like any other city during such an occasion of festive spirit, was completely decorated with colored flags and paper-leaves and was fully illuminated with colorful lamps. Beautiful, temporary arches were erected at all the entrances to the city. The streets were rapturous under a canopy of multi-colored flags of paper and cloth which fluttered in the gentle breeze.

I was going to the city together with my daughter and son who were studying in the primary school, in order to participate in the Grand Carnival. I was driving my car very slowly due to the rush and crowd in the street. My children were in an elite and excited mood, seeing the awkward dancing of the drunkards and hearing the music of the perspiring bandsmen.

Suddenly, from somewhere, a street-dog jumped to the front of my car. I stopped my car, kicking hard at the brake-pedal. My children pushed open the door of the car and rushed out, feeling great anxiety over the incident.

The street-dog, sitting by the side of my car, was licking at its raised fore-legs and was mildly howling in severe pain. Its fore-paws were crushed under the front wheel of my car. Holding up its fore-legs as if to greet us in the Indian fashion, it howled and moaned intermittently and licked at the bruised paws.   Evidently, it was suffering from severe pain and unbearable agony.   Seeing that sorrowful sight, both my children began to cry aloud.

A traffic policeman came towards me and ordered me rudely to remove the car from the road.  Though I compelled my children to get into the car; they turned a deaf ear to my pleadings.   They simply stood on the road, consoling that wounded street-dog.  And that lean, skeleton-like dog, keeping its scantly-haired tail in between its rear-legs, was still howling and moaning, as if demanding some compensation from me!

The policeman again yelled and roared to keep away the car from the road.  Both my children carried that street-dog gently and placed it on the backseat of the car, in between them.  The angry policeman began to laugh aloud, seeing the ridiculous situation into which I had fallen.

My children pleaded with me, or rather compelled me to drive the car to the nearest veterinary hospital.  They had already forgotten everything about the Grand Carnival.  Thus, dismissing all the programs of the festival, and cursing my own fate, we drove to the veterinary hospital and treated that hell of a dog.  With a feeling of comfort and safety, the street-dog began to wag its tail at me in gratitude, as if I were a Good Samaritan!

Later, though I asked my children to leave that street-dog somewhere there in the hospital premises or in the street, they refused to do so due to their compassion and mercy towards that mute, nay pitiable, creature. Sitting in the car, they had already begun to caress the dog and play with it. In fact, that street-dog had plucked at their heartstrings, or rather, had stolen their heart! It licked their hands and legs, smacked and wagged its tail unnecessarily and purred in gratitude.

My children shed tears of happiness and pointed out to me that its love is genuine and spotless. They patted on its head, exclaiming how grateful it was! Whatsoever, I brought it home quite reluctantly.

On reaching home, my children competed with each other in giving the street-dog milk and biscuits. It rapaciously gormandized on whatever was given to it, and looked up at their faces with an expression of legal right for more and more eatables!

I cleverly and carefully selected the name 'Nausea' for it because of its greedy behavior and ugly looks. But when my children, considering its unquenchable desire for milk, called it 'Inko', following the children's name for milk, I frankly suggested in an angry voice that 'Stinko' would be a better name. However, they began to call it Inko and I called it Nausea.

Within a week or two, its paws were healed and it began to run here and there in all our rooms quite freely. Precisely, it stayed about a year with us enjoying all sorts of royal treat and palatial facilities.

Day by day, during that period, my children were becoming leaner and leaner and that street-dog fatter and fatter. I was too late to realize that Nausea, pretending love to my children, was swallowing all the nourishing food I gave to my kids.

The Grand Carnival of August with all its colors and lights came to the city once again. My children and myself, all dressed up for the festival, got into the car. Surprisingly enough, Nausea came towards us from somewhere, and jumped into the backseat of the car. As the children insisted, I agreed with some hesitation, to take the dog also to the Carnival. That fat dog sat together with my children always keeping an expression of innocence on its face, until our car crossed the decorated entrance of the city.

The city had been pretty crowded. The drunkards danced and the bandsmen played. On reaching the spot where the accident had occurred in the previous year, I applied the brake of my car, rather unconsciously. Within a split second, that fat dog jumped out of the car through the window!

Owing to my children's insistence, I stopped the car by the side of the road. Both of them got out of the car and tried their best to bring back the dog. My poor kids lovingly called its name and desperately offered pieces of cake and biscuits. But, that ungrateful creature stared at them with its fiery eyes, as if it were seeing them for the first time, and even barked and snarled at them, displaying its sharp teeth, with a sort of cruel expression on its face.

Suddenly a traffic policeman came there and ordered me rudely to take my car away. He pointed out that parking was not allowed there due to the crowded traffic. In a moment, I remembered the tone and tempo of his voice and we exchanged our bewildered looks recognizing each other. The policeman offered himself to help my children, as he remembered the tragic incident that had occurred at the same place the previous year.

But, by this time, a few other street-dogs also came to the help of Nausea. All of them together stared and barked at us and even scratched on the ground with their hind legs, as if they were taking revenge upon us. Soon, knowing that there was a policeman among us, they under the leadership of Nausea, pinned their tails between their hind legs and disappeared into some dark hideouts of the city.

The policeman consoled my children saying, "However you try, a millipede will not lie on the mattress!" Then, he tried to console me too, by saying, "A buffalo goes only to the buffalo-herd!" Someway, I managed to get my crying children into the car, and started the car saying a few words of thanks to the policeman.

As I was driving the car, my mind puzzled over the real meaning of freedom, and its various definitions. My children, sitting on the back seat of the car, were whispering to each other that the street-dog would come back again on the next Grand Carnival to place its paws under the wheel of the car, and then they could take revenge against it. I deeply thought over the whole incident, and realized a new meaning as well as a new definition to the word 'freedom'!

Sitting in the lap of Kangchendzonga, the Wanderer also was thinking over the same thing and realizing many facts, like that Erewhonian Merchant...

Freedom... Liberty... Independence... Emancipation...

What is freedom or who are free? You are born free but everywhere you are in chains!

You are born, without your prior knowledge, just like an accident, in some part of this earth and thinks that it belongs to you and you only! You are born into a particular racial section or religious community or cultural denomination or language group and you feel elite! Others also think like you and there comes conflict.

Who are free and who are not? The masters or the slaves? The employers or the employees? The nomads or the highwaymen? The educated or the illiterate? Who should rule and who should be ruled? Who are superior and who are inferior? Who are the interrogators and who are the victims? In your own country, among your own people, you may experience slavery!

The Wanderer remembered the song of an Indian citizen from the southern most tip of the peninsula, which came to him like a lamentation from a far off place:

Please believe me, Sir, I'm an Indian;
more Indian than any other Indian;
a pure Indian among the numerous,
though unlucky to take birth,
on the wrong side of the track,
sans a gold-spoon in the mouth!

Then, a few interjections…! The cruel interrogation began; the strange question-answer session followed:

Oh shit! You claim an Indian…?
Your profile is not Indian…!
(You look like a Madrassi…)
Your complexion is not Indian…!
(For yours is Dravidian…)
Your dress is not Indian…!
(For you tuck up your dhoti…!)
You don't eat wheat chapathi…!
(Though we imposed our wheat and language,
you eat only rice dosai and iddli…!)

The primary round was over and, then, to the more serious questioning, exceeding all the limits of patriotism:

Your name is not Indian...!
(It is Macedonian...)
Your language is not Indi...!
(It's mere shit, Malam...malam...)
Your religion is not Indu...!
(It's of the Middle East...)
Your culture is not Indian...!
(For you have no Indian superstitions and false beliefs)
And shit, you claim an Indian...?

And the final words of pleadings of a helpless citizen who was turned a stranger in his own motherland by his own people:

But believe me, Sir, I'm an Indian,
With Indian blood and passport
Number: L 851963, issued at: 'Luck Now!'

But one cannot be lucky always! It doesn't matter whether you're an Indian or a Chinese, an Arabian or a German, an American or a Russian; all are one and the same in their predicaments! Religions create dilemmas for citizens in the name of gods, while in Politics, the gods are communism, totalitarianism, capitalism, democracy and dictatorship. The question is how long one can be docile or passive to a political or religious system. There's a limit for placidity; if you are a human being; even a harmless worm may turn into a venomous serpent when there is no other way of escape!

Even in Erewhon I was not free; I was not lucky, perhaps! The Wanderer thought. To be considered a stranger in one's own country is the severest punishment a citizen can be given!

To be imprisoned for uncommitted crimes! Words like freedom, liberty and independence are merely hackneyed ones, unless there is the Music of the Flute in the heart.

Whatever may be the definition of freedom, the wild rapture and the gentle happiness tendered by it cannot be explained. It goes deep into the heart of hearts like a flute - music; it stirs the body, mind and soul...

Where did I hear that Music of the Flute? Was it not at Erewhon? Or, did it become audible to me while lying exhausted, keeping my head on the bosom of Goddess Mumbai?

But then...?

The Wanderer tried to connect together the broken threads of a past dream. Lying on his sack-couch, he tried to recollect the old Music of the Flute...

Then... was not that Flute broken into pieces? Had not that Music ended for ever and ever?

Now, while resting on the lap of Kangchendzonga, how does this music happen to come here? From where does this Music of the Flute flow to my ears?

Maybe from the shepherd who looks after his sheep in the valley! I can clearly see him sitting on that hard rock, smoothened by Time. The flock of sheep is moving along the green valley like bundles of white cotton. And their joy doubles when they find new shoots of grass.

If only this Music of the Flute would never end! If only it could continue to blow forever and a day...

The Wanderer heaved a hot sigh. He tried to forget the past. He wished that the past should vanish into oblivion, and the present should become a part of the future. He slowly slipped into a reverie...

Later... Later... He took his chisel, brandished it and began to peck on a new piece of granite...

The Music of the Flute...

When it flowed from the hilltop, passing the woods, crossing the valley, crossing the river and passing the paddy-fields, and when it reached the town, I said in ecstasy, "Ha! The Music of the Flute...! It has the power to rejuvenate and to offer a new, hopeful life!"

Yes! The Music of the Flute...

It paused for a while in front of the City's Slaughterhouse and hanged around the piles of rotten flesh and the pools of stagnant blood.

Can the Music of the Flute prevent the stench of the Slaughterhouse?

The Slaughterer...

What attracted him was only the Odor of Death in that Music of the Flute. He paced unsteadily and his body swayed at every step. He walked forward seeking the origin of the Music of the Flute, passing the paddy-fields, crossing the river, crossing the valley and passing the woods...

The Slaughterer loved the unpleasant, horrid sound that was produced when the wind blew among the thick groves of reeds by the riverside. But when those reeds were cut, dried and notched, and when the Shepherd blew through it, the sound then produced by it nauseated him. For, it was then that the

Sheep kept for slaughtering, bleated aloud, hearing the Music of the Flute.

The Sheep...

The Sheep that silently stood in the Slaughterhouse, bowing their heads and cursing their inevitable fate! The Slaughterer knew that they stood with bowed heads because the Black Worms wriggled in their brains. He had patiently waited to watch the Black Worms writhe and flounce out of the brain when the separated head of the sheep was put in the fire before being cleansed for making soup. And the head of the sheep with the Black Worms in it was not at all good for soup!

But, that Music of the Flute! When it strained into the Slaughterhouse, the Sheep that stood with bowed heads would raise their heads and, looking up at the hilltop, start bleating. Perhaps, the Black Worms would have been wriggling and struggling in their brains then!

Can the Music of the Flute destroy the Black Worms in the brain?

The Music of the Flute...

Seeking its origin, the Slaughterer waddled here and there on the hilltop. He looked for it among the woods and behind the rocks. At last, at the end of that long search...

The Shepherd...

The Slaughterer found the Shepherd sitting on a smooth rock, deeply immersed in the Music of the Flute, forgetting everything else. The Sheep were leaping and dancing around him; the Sheep with Black Worms in their brains!

The Slaughterer gulped a mouthful of saliva and murmured, "Ah! The fatted Sheep!"

There, the Shepherd, his back double-bent by feeding the Sheep! He was blowing the flute, forgetful of even himself. He continued playing the flute, ignoring the presence of the Slaughterer.

"There maybe the Black Worms wriggle and struggle in his brain too," said the Slaughterer to himself.

The Sheep cared neither for the Shepherd nor for the Slaughterer but for the Music of the Flute! Ignoring the surroundings, they danced and leapt in the intoxication of the Music that flowed from the Flute!

The smell of the fatted Sheep maddened the Slaughterer. He roared aloud, "Stop it! That damned Music of the Flute!"

The Music of the Flute suddenly stopped. The dancing of the Sheep too ended abruptly. They began to walk with bowed heads as there were Black Worms in their brains!

"Hey, Shepherd! Will you give me these fatted sheep?" the Slaughterer asked greedily.

The Shepherd shook his head and said, "No! Never! I won't give my Sheep for slaughtering; I nurtured them dearly not to give away for slaughter."

The Slaughterer gnashed his teeth, quivered with rage, and breathed fire and fury. He approached the Shepherd like a lecher voluptuously seducing a virgin to quench his lust. He pulled out the slaughter-knife from its sheath that was fastened to the belt around his waist.

The Sheep that carried the Black Worms in their brains, walked away with their bowed heads, looking for new grass shoots!

"No! No! Never," the Shepherd cried adamantly.

The Slaughterer roared like a wild beast that found its prey. With the Slaughter-knife, he struck the Shepherd on his head.

The skull of the Shepherd was split. He fell down on that smooth rock, writhed in agony and died. The Flute that was separated from his loosened grip fell on the ground. From the gory gash on his head came out Black Worms, wriggling and writhing; the Black Worms that gnawed at the brains of the Sheep...

From the hilltop, the Slaughterer with the sinister smile of Cain, the first murderer, walked down the valley, guiding the Sheep that lost the real leader. The sheep, with the Black Worms in their brains, walked through the woods, nibbling at the new grass-shoots...

Then, the Shearer...

He came up to the woods, passing the paddy-fields, crossing the river and crossing the valley. When the Slaughterer saw him, fear raised its head in him like a hooded snake.

The Shearer, who actually came up to see the Shepherd, watched with desire the Sheep led by the Slaughterer.

Looking at the Sheep that walked with bowed heads like living bundles of fleece, the Shearer delightfully said, "Wow! Look, how fast the wool grows on them! Yes, the wool of the Sheep grows fast if only they hear the Music of the Flute!"

The Slaughterer shook his head in disgust and said, "Hey! Shearer! Don't utter even a word about the Shepherd or about the Music of the Flute. Now, let's do one thing. Why can't we both come to an understanding? You shear the Sheep and take the wool. What I want is only its meat."

Both of them walked down the valley with bowed heads, together leading the Sheep. Perhaps, the Black Worms were wriggling in their brains too!

The Sheep walked on with bowed heads! Crossing the valley, crossing the river and passing the paddy-fields, towards the City's Slaughterhouse...

The Sheep that stood in the Slaughterhouse did not bleat as they were not hearing the Music of the Flute from the hilltop. They, bearing the Black Worms in their brains, stood silently with bowed heads, waiting for each one's turn...

Is the Silence more meaningful than the Music of the Flute?

I, with head held high, started walking from the City, passing the paddy-fields, crossing the river, crossing the valley and passing the woods, towards the hilltop... seeking the Flute that lay by the side of the smooth rock, without anyone to blow it... blow through it... the eternal Music of the Flute... Ah!!

The reverie came to a stop. Far away from some hilltop, a solitary shepherd was still playing the flute. Being drowned in the heavenly Music of the Flute, the Wanderer sat like a stone-statue. He felt himself one among those numerous rocks of the valley, the silent auditors of the Music of the Flute!

But... Where does this search lead me? This eternal search...? Does it mean that the present is not at all different from the past?

Or... Is the presence of Black Worms inside the sheep's skull which makes them bow their heads merely a super-stition of some Nepali tribe who live in the lap of Kangchendzonga?

Or... Is it a fact that provokes the whole people of the world to think, and thereby, unveils the deception of their charlatan-rulers who keep the word of promise to the ear and break it to the hope?

Isn't it a truth quite sufficient to disclose the secret behind the declaration of mutual wars and, later, the signing of peace treaties by the rulers, purely for their self-motivated coexistence?

And Truth...! We usually know about it through our

experience! And experience...! It is not necessary that experience should come to us only through our five senses! One can experience Truth even through imagination.

Then... Why do some people accept a specific truth and some others oppose the same truth? Yes! It is quite natural that when the truth, that is realized by our sages through their own experience, reaches us in the course of time, we accept it through our own experience, and we oppose it as and when we fail to experience it. Yet we cannot stop plumbing the depth of things and so...

"Excuse me! I hope that you don't mind the introduction I gave you for conveying a truth that has been learned by me and my colleagues through our own experience!"

Who told me thus? Was it not that young laborer with sunken eyes, who stopped me somewhere in the streets of Erewhon and opened before me the casket of his experience with such an introduction?

For a moment, the Wanderer stopped to be a philosopher and tried to understand matters in the light of practicability. He realized the fact that he could never forget the visage of that Erewhonian coolie. The despair-stricken face of that poor laborer appeared on the silver screen of his mind. A representative of all the Erewhonian laborers who always wore a haggard and mournful look!

There was the light of truth in the words of that laborer. Those were sincere words coming out of the depth of emotion. And so his words must become a part of history, as they are...!

The Wanderer sharpened his chisel and started striking on

the stone. From fiction his chisel was gliding towards truth, the eternal truth...

When Pontius Pilate asked, "What is truth?" he did not care for the seriousness of that question. Perhaps, as Bacon suggested jesting Pilates would not stay for answers! But as that truth still exists, I would have to accept the old truth that 'Power corrupts and absolute power corrupts absolutely' only because I have been an ordinary citizen. Besides, am I only an average proletarian, discharging my duties honestly and punctually, though I am quite conscious of the fact that all my rights are merely on paper?

For the same reason, I am unable to conceal all the truths about that corrupted Tree of Life. Generally speaking, I am not an inherent hater of trees and, as a matter of fact, my ancestors were all lovers of trees from time immemorial. Yet, I am not foolish enough to love a corrupted, spreading tree with the full awareness of the fact that thousands may die under it when it falls down uprooted!

You could well imagine how proud we were while telling each other that our manufactory has the fifth place in size among all other factories of the world and is second only to another factory in the number of its laborers! But it is highly regrettable to say that none of us did not realize how we, while working mechanically in our manufactory for a pretty long period, were turned into machines or the machines on which we were working all these years, were transformed into us!

It was the age of male supremacy and so, no one was there

to threaten us or force us to work. Labor was then a natural instinct with us! But, as the Women's Liberation Movement began to spread its roots, naturally we, who were mere shovels under the system of democracy, had to welcome the new machine called the Tree of Life into our manufactory.

Even still I remember how we had greeted the Tree of Life, which was adored and worshipped by us all these years even otherwise, and welcomed it into the manufactory with great rejoice, love and respect. The Tree of Life with its dignified size and shape, its soft trunk, its two fat but round roots, its two long but lean branches and its twigs with dark-green leaves, aroused uncontrollable rapture and unlimited hope in us.

Are we not real fools who expected fruits in abundance from that Tree of Life which had already proven its incapability of giving at least a single fruit even to Adam, the First Man? To say it clearly, we the innocent and hard working laborers, at first, did not notice the black, sticky Water of Life that was spontaneously flowing through a cleft, or rather a split, on the soft and lovely trunk, in between the two fat-round roots of the Tree of Life. However, the Controllers of the factory had come to know about it and were exploiting the opportunity, without bringing it to the notice of the laborers.

Even if taking the scanty power of the laborers into consideration, the Tree of Life was under my authority for I have been working in this factory ever since its inception. However, when the Tree of Life, gradually and systematically, acquired an equal position with me, I realized the truth that power, however less it is, will corrupt.

And by then, the Tree of Life had become too puissant and had grown beyond my control! The poor helpless laborers of the factory, including myself, had to continue our work watching indifferently at the cleft that widened gradually in between the two roots of the Tree of Life as well as at the

Controllers of the factory who worked under the sedative-ness caused by the toxic effect of the Water of Life that was oozing out of it.

By and by, the Tree of Life began to capture the whole powers of the manufactory, one by one. We the laborers, being 'hostile to the past, impatient of the present, and cheated of the future' as Camus says, pushed on our days by fearfully delivering our duties which occupied our body and absorbed our mind, and by desperately realizing that the papers on which we had scribbled the dream of our rights were slipping away from our hands and the solid sandbank of human-rights was washed from under our feet and by hopelessly worrying what would be the future of this factory that had been erected and established with our own blood and sweat. We silently pulled our socks up just to keep our body and soul together!

In short, the Tree of Life took over the absolute power of the factory with the passage of time and, thereby, began to make the old Controllers as well as the ordinary laborers like us, work hard like galley-slaves! Alas! We were then the gigolos of a corrupted tree!

By then, the Tree of Life which gained whatever it had wished for began itself to wither away. The cleft in between its roots reduced to a tiny crack and the flow of the Water of Life through it came to a stop. Its trunk lost softness, its roots and branches dried and its lovely bark wrinkled and its leaves on the twigs turned 'yellow, and black, and pale, and hectic red' to quote Shelley. But, what could we, the laborers do, as we were paralyzed and numbed in our body and mind under the heavy weight of the yoke that was thrust upon our necks by the Tree of Life, and of the shackles that bound our hands and legs?

However, we the laborers, including myself, could realize through our own experience the truth that 'power corrupts and absolute power corrupts absolutely.' Just that's all…!

**I**s that all? Oh, No! Think of the final fall. 'Ah, what a fall!' Every autocrat has a fall! The only difficulty is that we have to wait patiently until his or her star descends.

When a person gives witness from his own experience, how can you disbelieve it? Of course, when mere laborers vouch for the truth, their language may be handicapped. Even then, experience will ever remain as truth at least to the person concerned.

With an ordinary person language is often insufficient. And he does not know the numerous tricks and twists applied in language. He even does not know how to bring out his own experience of truth through suitable symbols. And there, we seek the help of the intelligentsia!

But what could the helpless members of the public do when the intelligentsia, from whom we expect a lot, stand akimbo in sheer indifference or rather in mere idleness? These intellectuals, who even claim themselves as literary men, are really a curse to history! And that is exactly what the young Erewhonian whom I had met somewhere in Erewhon, also told me.

The Wanderer tried to fan the embers till he had that humorous story of the young Erewhonian at his finger's ends. When the stone, on which he had carved the laborer's testimony of truth, was rolling down into the valley, the Wanderer selected a new piece of granite and began to peck on it. While recollecting the story, he felt light hearted, and a smile was lingering in between his lips.

We can very well understand when the First-Man who was quite helpless and forlorn, imitated the Bow-wow language for the first time. But what can be done if, literary men who consider themselves as intellectuals, stand aside, even in this modern age, proclaiming, "Alas, the language is insufficient today!" instead of trying to develop the language into a suitable media of expressing all genuine thoughts and feelings? We can also understand if they are lazing away their life just after turning the language into their monopoly. But how long...? How long can we forgive these litterateurs who injure and irritate the whole of humanity by presenting the subject matter through the easy means of symbols? How sad it is, if we, who are impatiently waiting for a chance to make the moon our habitat, still imitate the 'Ding-dong' language of trees, plants and creepers? Their lackadaisical approach to the language is not only horrible but unpardonable as they disturb our generally accepted system of reasoning! Woe betide!

Well, I became quite aware of this erosion of language that had happened to the modern man, when I had an opportunity to talk with a so-called litterateur hailing from my native place. When that lanky man, with his long beard and disheveled hair, wearing the hypocritical Khaddar dhoti and knee-touching kurta, slowly walked from the other end of the street and approached me, I brought an incident that had happened a few minutes before to his notice. And the incident was just like this:

A healthy black hound and a fat white pig, chasing the former, suddenly, from somewhere, appeared in the street. The spectacle of the hound that was running frantically, being ignorant of its own strength, as well as of the white pig that was following the former, joggling its folds of flesh and snorting with rage, gave us much food for laughter.

Then… All of a sudden the scene shifted and the atmosphere changed! As the hound was trying to cross the road, a fast moving car knocked it down to the other side of the road! It was lying there by the side of the road, quite formidably with its broken backbone, its chain of intestine thrusting out through the burst-open stomach and its ears vibrating in obvious pain.

No need to say that the white pig which was following the black hound also crossed the road. Suddenly, a government vehicle that passed like lightning ran over it too! For a moment the vehicle slowed down and, then, accelerated into its usual speed towards its destination. The hind legs as well as the buttocks of the white pig had been smashed to the ground. Yet, it snorting wrathfully crawled on its fore legs towards the dead hound and voraciously swallowed its chain of entrails!

Then, with a cruel thirst, the white pig quickly lapped up all the blood that was oozing into the stomach of the black hound. Then only we, the spectators, noticed a horrible fact! The blood that formed a pool in the stomach of the black hound was actually the blood that was oozing out of the white pig's own snout! That foolish white pig, being ignorant of this truth, was quite happy in getting more and more blood to drink. Forgetting the horror of death that was straining into its soul, and enjoying the momentary satisfaction from the warm blood of the black hound, that nincompoop of a white pig, drowned itself into a sort of bliss…

And then…

The litterateur, who was hearing my narration of this simple and ordinary accident, in his ecstasy made this laconic expletive: "Ha! What a symbolic incident!!"

Look! How the language becomes insufficient! I wonder why couldn't these litterateurs stop their writing and lead a happy domestic life with their spouses and kids! If they could produce two or three children more that itself would turn leastwise, to be a credit to the man-power of this world!

Anybody can understand the seriousness of that Erewhonian's indignation. Those who are unchangeable... those who do not want to be changed... and those who blindly oppose or raise silly objections when changes come naturally! How many types of people! Variety thy name is Man!

The Wanderer's mind was wandering in the wilderness. He failed to anchor his brain at some safe flanks. He sat there silently allowing his brain to work as much as it could...

Evolution... if not revolution... change! That is inevitable! And that's the need of Time! When a change is necessary, it must come in its own natural way. For good or bad, a change or rather an evolution is highly essential...

"Most of us criticized Charles Darwin when he, through his Evolution Theory, established that all creatures from Amoeba to Man underwent fundamental physical changes due to the shift in environments."

Where did I hear this preface-like sentence? Is it not a young Erewhonian who told me the wonderful story of a typical evolution, with this very same introduction?

The smile on the face of the Wanderer vanished suddenly. The words of the young Erewhonian echoed in his ears. He began to recollect that typical story.

Yes! He narrated that story just like a grandma who was telling a mysterious fairytale to her great-grand-children. And so, this tale also must become a landmark in history...

The Wanderer took his chisel and began pecking on a new piece of granite...

"Most of us criticized Charles Darwin... and... who would not have wondered..."

Who would not have wondered at these physical changes of the creatures, when they shifted their place of living from water to land and from land to air? We could not believe so easily that the fins used for swimming in the water were changed into legs, and the hands used for climbing up the trees were changed into feathered wings for flying in the air. We have begun to realize that the tail was shortened to naught and the trunk shrank into nose or the teeth grew into tusks and horns. However, as the doubt still prevails whether such unconscious changes, for the survival of the species in accordance with the shift in the environment, occurred accidentally or gradually, the evolution really came as an undeniable fact to that government officer who was working just under our noses!

When I say a government officer, do not misunderstand that he was a fellow of the Erewhonian Administrative Service or a green-ink-user who controlled some state-secretariat! As we all know, he was only a mere traffic policeman!

How many years had his name been on the muster-roll of the Employment Exchange, as a procedural matter! But, had he not got that government job as a result of giving money, that he acquired by selling his father's only piece of land, as a bribe to some minister's notorious Private Secretary, when the numerous tests and interviews he had attended turned futile? And how suddenly he, who had been queuing under the scorching sun for many days to get the allowance of the unemployed, became a government employee!

After the successful completion of his training, he was appointed in an ordinary town to control the traffic of a junction where only three roads met. On the very day of his assignment, he began to stop the vehicles that were coming from the two roads and to allow the vehicles of the third one to pass, by showing a beckoning-sign with his raised chin. Every two minutes, he shifted his position so as to allow other vehicles to pass, and this 'stop and pass' game continued for years. Though the muscles of his hands became strong and muscle-bound due to this constant, devotional work, the muscles and veins of his neck misplaced themselves in their continuous to and fro movements and, gradually, his neck became elastic like a rubber tube!

Days and months passed like that. By then, he had become

an indivisible part of that junction of three roads. His head and hands moved like an automatic machine. Even when he was fast asleep, his head moved sideways on the pillow. As both his hands moved up and down in his sleep, they usually hurt by striking on the bedsteads or against the walls. See! How pathetic is the condition of a sincere government employee!

However, when the government declared a state of Emergency, it brought a thorough change in his life. He was promoted from that ordinary town's junction of three roads to a big city's junction of four roads. Though the burden of work increased proportionately, he was happy in getting appropriate salary and power as well as the infallibility which was quite evident in the declaration of Emergency. And the Emergency, as everybody knew, was an immunization against all moral obligations!

He was in utter confusion, at first, when he came to the junction of four roads, as he was only familiar with a junction of three roads where he simply had to stop the vehicles with two hands and to allow other vehicles to pass with a beckoning sign of his head. But, when he realized that the stopping of vehicles is more important than allowing them to pass, then and there, the movement of his head stopped forever!

Thence forward, he stopped with both his hands all the vehicles that came by the three roads. And the vehicles that came along the fourth road stopped for a moment in front of him without knowing what to do and, later, passed the traffic umbrella after throwing coins into the pocket of the policeman who was standing there like a statue!

As days passed, the weight of his pocket increased and he altered the size of his pocket accordingly. Soon, he bought a plot of land in the heart of the city and built a splendid mansion there and, later, he bought even a rubber estate in his native village, giving only a meager amount.

The traffic of the city was increasing day by day. The stopping of the vehicles that came one by one to throw coins into his pocket began to create much traffic problems in that junction of four roads. Therefore, those who owned vehicles began coming to his mansion to hand over the amount directly, on a monthly basis. Now, it became a part of his responsibility that such vehicles should be allowed to pass whenever they came to the junction. And fortunately, appropriate evolutionary development occurred to him in accordance with the change of the environment. He felt a kind of lesion on his face and his nose began to grow considerably!

When it grew like the trunk of an elephant, to a length of two and a half feet, fingers began to appear at its tip. As a very clever police officer, he used that opportunity and placed the 'STOP' board among the newly grown fingers. Maybe this government officer was the disciple of that unscrupulous man in the Malayalam saying who considered the growth of a banyan tree at his anus to be a comfortable shade for him! Yet, we must admit that the evolution that came to the traffic policeman helped a lot to avoid the difficulties in controlling traffic in that junction of four roads.

And if this much evolution could come to an ordinary traffic policeman, according to the situation which existed during the Emergency, we could well guess the changes that had occurred to all other government employees, including the so-called green-inked officers, from peons to panjandrums!

The Wanderer's face beamed as if he had discovered a great truth. He brooded over the pros and cons of the Emergency that was declared in Erewhon...

Changes come to a certain extent even without anybody's efforts. And a situation in which a government is compelled to enforce the black laws of Emergency may occur at any time in all the countries of the world. There is nothing to be surprised about it. But it is a shock to think about the Emergency in Erewhon! Because the only country where the Law of Emergency is declared in the name of progress and development of the nation would be none but Erewhon! Or how could a democratic government declare Emergency when the majority of the citizens suspect the fidelity of their policies? Only foolish autocrats would take such drastic steps, and it would be merely for their own survival in power. And when they die, the whole world will curse them and make them their laughing stock!

And alas! Samuel Butler's Erewhon is changed into such a country! Everything here moves under a spell of beastliness! Brutes rule the Man! The situation presented by Jonathan Swift is coming to a reality here in Erewhon. The story of the man who becomes quite helpless or pretends to be helpless before mere horses! How prophetic Swift is!

And the story does not end even there! The Animal Farm of George Orwell is nothing but this Erewhon! There may be change in persons but the situation is the same. There is no change even in the method of administration! Except for the fact that the Wheel of Time has rolled forward, Erewhon is undoubtedly the Animal Farm.

The Wanderer tried to evaluate Erewhon under this new

idea of transfiguration. His mind made a hurried survey of certain latent facts concerning Erewhon which had been transformed into Orwell's Animal Farm. With a languishing look, he sat silently under the lambent sky. Then, screwing up his energy, he began to peck on a new piece of granite...

It is true that many a year had passed since the white pig Mister Jones and his family left this Animal Farm! But after that, had it not been here the autocratic rule of the brown pig Napoleon who had taken over the power from them? And was it not the faithful followers of Napoleon who had shot down and killed Snowball who had labored day in and day out to evict Mister Jones and his family out of this Farm?

Almost all the animals of this Farm recognized Napoleon, as he was capable of accusing Mister Jones for anything and everything. And then, one day Napoleon died and his only daughter Napoleona took over the rule of the Animal Farm. Thereby the situation in the Animal Farm turned out to be just like the Malayalam saying, 'the cow died and the buttermilk lost all its sourness.'

All the expectations of the animals were shattered and all their dreams burned to ashes! And the animals of the Farm who had feared the whip and suffered the flogging of Mister Jones, had really forgotten what exactly should be done. They spent their days bearing all the injustice silently and deciding to suffer patiently whatever might happen.

It was a hobby for Napoleona that she formed hundreds and thousands of Committees and Commissions and Corporations in the name of progress, to exploit the people. Yet, she always tried to please the people by telling them that the emblem of the Farm that was moving towards the next century would always be animals.

And the donkeys called the public, or rather vice versa, stood aside just like spectators without joining sides or supporting any particular group. Encouraging those successors of Benjamin, Napoleona would say repeatedly in all her public meetings, "Don't regret that you are all donkeys, for only donkeys have longevity."

And when Napoleona left a particular place, addressing a series of public meetings at selected spots of the Animal Farm, the successors of Benjamin would collect their meal-packets from the party office concerned and say belching, "Computer or no computer, life will continue just like in old days, in its worst condition."

It was really intolerable for Napoleona to step down from power and leave its glory. She blindly believed that her family-line was ever created to rule this Farm. She persuaded Squealers, who were slaves and sycophants of her family, to speak to the members of the public. Whenever they got a platform, they addressed the citizens and said, "Friends, Animals, Countrymen, lend me your ears! Don't even fancy that leadership is such an interesting thing. It is simply a heavy and deep obligation! And Napoleona takes all the decisions herself because she knows if the decisions are left to her colleagues they are likely to go wrong. What's needed here is discipline, steel-like discipline! Or else, our enemies and traitors may occupy this Farm at any moment. Therefore, tactics are always essential, anywhere and everywhere."

The innocent auditors, who were incapable of realizing that these types of public addresses were simply a part of those deceitful tactics by which they were cheated of their birthrights, once again praised Napoleona and even sympathized at her great sacrifice in bearing the heavy weight of the crown and the scepter.

The successors of the cart-horses, Clover and Boxer, suppressed their sorrow, seeing and hearing all that were happening around them. By shedding tears at the sad plight of their Farm, they worked hard and bore heavy loads. They recollected those wonderful hopes they had when they drove Mister Jones out of this Farm. It was true that things were much better than in those yesteryears. But was it only for these much change that their ancestors had shown their broad chests in front of the bullets that came from the guns of Mister Jones?

Napoleona, the present ruler, was not only beautiful but also clever or rather cunning. Whenever she felt that the subjects were turning against her, she took some or other steps to distract their attention. Or she exploited the situation by spreading rumors that the neighboring Farm was making preparations for an unexpected attack!

In order to hide her own inability to solve the internal problems of the Farm, Napoleona used to make certain aphoristic slogans and axioms and they were inscribed on the walls of public buildings. She created a number of maxims and epigrams like 'Work more, talk less,' 'Work hard, earn more, but spend less,' 'Real happiness comes from hard work,' 'A child is a heavy burden,' 'If there is no child, there is no problem,' etcetera.

Moreover, Napoleona used to say in public meetings, "Do you know why I work hard day in and day out? It's for you and for the progress of our Farm."

Then, the voice of someone would rise up from the audience, "What the hell are you doing all these years?"

And she would retort in a pleasing tone, "We spend our restless days and sleepless nights by moving files, making reports, preparing minutes and writing memoranda."

Again, someone else would yell from the crowd, with an air of suspicion, "But... could those papers save us from poverty and starvation?"

Napoleona would then reply in a prayer-like manner, "Look! Poverty, suffering and despair are the unchangeable laws of life. They are a part of our fate and so we must suffer them silently and patiently. However, sooner or later, all these sufferings will end and that beautiful day of our dream, the wonderful day of equality, fraternity and liberty will come. Perhaps, that will not happen in your span of life, yet, there is no reason to doubt the arrival of such a good-day."

"But, while the majority of us in this Farm are suffering without proper food, clothing or shelter, a few among us are leading a luxurious life. How long could we tolerate such an injustice?" Someone would murmur in utter despair.

Soon Napoleona would take out the Constitution of the Farm, which had undergone useless amendments from time to time, and would read aloud with great enthusiasm, "See! Here our sages wrote like this! 'All are equal! But some are more equal than others.'

She would continue her speech, after a meaningful pause, "We can go forward only with this Constitution. And all those who oppose it or doubt its sanctity and sanity are but traitors! That's what I say, 'Mere traitors!'"

However, a few intelligent donkeys were still murmuring, "Look! Your final collapse is certain. You swop horses in midstream and so your doom is sealed!"

And how could fundamental changes come for this Animal Farm? For the members of this Farm are not facing a problem that can be solved simply by making a new agreement with Mister Pilkington instead of the earlier one with Mister Jones!

Who can say that changes are not occurring? But, what is the use of such changes if each one of them turns to be a new shackle to chain the people? Here, one can very well come to a certain syllogism. And there is no need to ponder over the answer of two plus two! Perhaps, this may be the fate of all these Yahoos!

And there are periodical historians who always try to establish that all such changes are for the benefit of the people! Napoleona was only a Pig in a particular animal farm but what about hundreds of other animal farms ruled by other animals like Cow, Donkey, Elephant or Lion? They all claim that they change the style or place of their domination for the interest of the subjects! Take the history of any country in the world and check for yourself. There you can find a list of hidden facts, or rather, facts which are purposefully hidden! And take, for instance, the history of India...

The pictures of various kings and emperors passed through the mind of the Wanderer. The glorious and inglorious reigns of a myriad of rulers lingered in his mind.

Those who brought changes... Those who tried to bring changes but failed miserably... Those who proved that changes however foolish were for the benefit of the subjects... And those who never cared to bring any kind of change...!

For a moment the period of Mohammed-bin Tughlak from the history of India filled his mind. He realized that it was his duty to write a gloss or rather a footnote to that limited historical record.

Yes! It is the need of the age! For those historians who highlighted the shifting of the capital as one of the most progressive steps of Mohammed-bin Tughlak, purposefully ignored certain basic facts concerning this exclusive whim of that atypical emperor. And so, it must be disclosed as additional information to the students of Indian history!

The Wanderer took a new stone. He burnished his chisel and started pecking on it with great concentration, as it was the truthful outcome of his long contemplation...

Mohammed-bin Tughlak is perhaps the most interesting character to those students who study Indian History. Though he had certain good hereditary qualities, his incapability to implement *his* ideals, his cruel and inhuman approach to those who opposed him, his blind faith in those who supported and praised him and, above all, his hot temper, blood thirst and flesh-love made him a fool of history. At the same time he was a scholar, a creative genius and was charitable and kind. It was perhaps, considering all these characteristics of his nature that Doctor Smith called him 'a mixture of opposites.'

Whatsoever, almost all the historians have stressed that his reign was notable for many reasons. His attempt to bring all neighboring countries and their peoples, varying in race, religion and language under him, his movement to introduce copper coins on which the picture of his own head was embossed and, above all, his efforts to shift the capital of his country from Delhi would have, perhaps, given Mohammed-bin Tughlak the eligibility for the 'Man of the Year' award, if such titles used to be in vogue in those days!

Though many a historian has pointed out a number of reasons behind the decision of Mohammed-bin Tughlak to shift his capital from Delhi, a main reason was the slums of the poor who swarmed in and around the city. Such slums not only marred the beauty of the capital city but also gave a severe headache to the Sultan. The Sultan who used to roam around the capital city in disguise, as part of his duty, to look after the 'well-being' of the belle damsels there, naturally felt headache, as his sacred head hit against the lintels of the small huts into which he had walked in. Because of this reason, he felt constant headache whenever he saw or even thought of such slums with low entrances where his poor subjects eked out their existence.

The intelligent Sultan had realized that if all the beautiful girls of the slums were brought one by one into his palace, there would not be much space left out! Moreover, if palaces were constructed and given to all the beauties with whom he had spent nights in dalliance, the royal treasury would soon become empty. It was in such a situation that the Sultan thought, for the first time, of the shifting of the capital from the slum-packed Delhi to Agra! Thus, he summoned the Royal Architect and entrusted him with the responsibility of building up the capital with all its corresponding palaces on the banks of the blue Jumna.

One day, as the construction of the new capital city was progressing, the Sultan came to Agra to see the work for himself. And while walking along the shores of the Jumna, he met a beautiful girl and forgot for a moment everything about the construction work of the capital city. On that night, as the Sultan was entering into the hut of that belle dame, his sacred head hit against the lintel of the front door and, thus, he suddenly realized the truth that there were slums in Agra too! On the very next day, the Sultan ordered that Agra was not suitable for the construction of the capital city and subsequently cut off the head of the palace-architect.

With the death of the Royal Architect, there were none left in the country capable of constructing a new capital city. And the slums of Delhi were creating much headache for the Sultan, again and again. That was how the Sultan together with his royal train went to Devagiri which was renamed by him as Daulatabad, sticking to the old saying, "Where there is the king and his train, there is the capital," even though special palaces were not constructed for the same. As the saying, "A king's order splits even a rock" still existed, all the people of Delhi except those who were living in slums, followed the Sultan to Devagiri. And, as you know very well, everything about that sad and miserable journey is clearly recorded in the yellow pages of Indian History.

On the very same day of the arrival of Mohammed-bin Tughlak in Devagiri, he walked along the streets to see for himself the well-being of his subjects. And as he was entering the hut of a beautiful girl whom he had met on the way, his sacred head collided against the lintel of the front door. Thus the Sultan, realizing that the slum-packed Devagiri too was not suitable for making his capital, on the very next day, ordered his train to go back to Delhi. Owing to utter starvation, untold hardships and indescribable miseries suffered by the people during their return journey, all the old people perished and all the young turned old. No wonder, within two or three days of their arrival in Delhi, the Sultan again began to feel headache!

Therefore, Mohammed-bin Tughlak issued an order to crush down all the huts and remove all the slums which not only gave him headache but also marred the beauty of his capital city. Then and there, the loyal guards and other conscience-keepers of the Sultan brought a number of elephants and began to pull down the huts and trample over them for the evacuation of the slums.

The little children, whose parents had gone in search of their daily bread, were sleeping peacefully in those huts and tents. They were all trampled to death under the big feet of the elephants. Those humanists who came to rescue the infants were threatened and chased away from that cauldron of official atrocity. The wailing and sobbing of the evacuees turned to be a mere cry in the wilderness. And then, the elephants were dancing over the huts where cheap food-materials, moldy eatables and semi-decayed vegetables, those things thrown away from the big shops of the city, were displayed and sold!

The Sultan himself came down to see the evacuation of the slums situated near the Great Gate through which his own ancestors entered or rather trespassed into Delhi. He even cajoled his flattering kinsmen and slavish coterie to rename those slum-cleared areas, giving new names like Tughlakpur and Tughlak Nagar, following the method he had adopted while changing the name of Devagiri into Daulatabad.

And some time later, being struck by the curses of the poor who had dwelt in the slums of Delhi, the Sultan, Mohammed-bin Tughlak, passed away, handing over the burden of rule to his successor. And as Lane Poole, the historian says: his reign was 'a tragedy of high intentions self-defeated.'

Mohammed-bin Tughlaks pass away, one by one! And their deaths give consolation to the subjects! And if they die of accidents, it is not merely a coincidence. Nature, in fact, is making fun of them!

But how could the students of history who had studied the maxim 'History repeats' feel comfort and solace? Never mind, for Mohammed-bin Tughlaks give them amusement and not grief!

Yes! In order to amuse the students of history, Mohammed-bin Tughlaks will continue to be reborn in each and every country!

The Wanderer fixed his eyes at the pinnacle of Kangchendzonga. He sighed heavily thinking about the various historical incidents that were recurring in the course of time...

How pitiable are the lives of those Royal Architects and Royal Doctors who sacrifice themselves for the sake of foolish Tughlaks! The juggernauts of royal idiosyncrasy! The innocent preys to the stupidity of rulers! Are they not mere termite-flies that slap into the holy fire-pits made by the rulers for their own benefits? And when fate boomerangs against these foot-lickers who, according to their own estimate, toil and trouble and strain every nerve to save their country somehow, who is there to rescue them from their inevitable doom? And that exactly is what happened to the palace doctor of Erewhon!

The typical incident narrated in the case-diary of an Erewhonian Psychiatrist passed through the mind of the Wanderer. He had come across it during his stay in Erewhon. He began to inscribe the incident, as it was given in the diary, on a new piece of granite...

Our palace doctor was a person who always thought concretely and practically over the future of the nation. Gradually, he realized that the only way to solve the major problems of our country, like unemployment and scarcity of food, was to prevent overpopulation.

He had no doubt that if the present rate of population grew proportionately, the public life in this country would become quite unbearable by the first half of the next century. Moreover, unwieldy crowds had already become an ordinary spectacle in every nook and corner of the country.

A number of small houses and huts had already been erected even on good, fertile lands. Yet, the palace doctor was surprised at the fact that the people of this country, who were generally lazy and particularly opposed to the idea of manual labor, had been defeating other countries just in the matter of producing more children!

This uncontrollable increase in population not only destroyed the financial system of this country but also upturned its planning schemes. He believed that if things were going on like this, much time would not be taken for the total destruction of this country. He always brooded over the matter, worrying what a palace doctor could do in saving the country from such a fatal doom.

At last, collecting the maximum available statistics and demographic records on the matter, he prepared a treatise, explaining how the increase in population was harmful to the progress of the country, and it was presented before the king. The king who was worried of his own incapability in implementing an economic system suitable for solving the country's problems, gave great importance to the treatise and came to the conclusion that 'Population' is not 'Man Power' but merely a 'Great Problem.' Moreover, he appointed an all-powerful Enquiry Commission to find out the causes and remedies for the increase of population as well as to implement proper remedial measures immediately, and the palace doctor was ordered to be the Chairman of the Commission.

The Court of Enquiry traveled throughout the country in chariots and palanquins as well as on horses and elephants, and collected evidence. Later, the Commission presented before the king, on time, its report containing all its findings.

The following were the major issues, which received special emphasis in the report of the Enquiry Commission. First of all, to give birth to the maximum number of children is a holy rite in this country, just like mendicancy and nudity. Secondly, the women of this country, who are illiterate and are working hard in kitchens under their mothers-in-law, utilize every opportunity to attain pregnancy, as an easy way to get rest and respect. Thirdly, the fact that every child born has only one mouth to eat but two hands to work is a consolation to all heads of the poor families. Fourthly, those parents having only girl-children or boy-children tend to continue their experiments with self-assertion and optimism till a coveted boy-child or girl-child is born to them. Fifthly, if sex education were given to the adolescents of this tropical country, they would become parents even before attaining the age of maturity, and thereby, the population of this country would increase unconditionally. Sixthly, even if Myrobolan Trees or *Terminalia Chebula* were planted as part of the Forest Festival, it would help only a minority who have taken the oath of celibacy because only young celibates used the *ayurvedic* potion made from *Chilbulic Myrobolan* cones to keep their sexual instinct down. Seventhly and lastly, owing to the above reasons, only compulsory sterilization through vasectomy or tubectomy could solve the population problem of this country.

Reading the Enquiry Commission's report of activities, the king embraced the palace doctor with uncontrollable joy, and even gave his beautiful, only daughter in marriage to him. Thus, the king bestowed his signet-ring upon the palace doctor who had lately become his son-in-law, and blessed him by sanctioning nineteen months' supreme authority to use any fair or foul method for controlling the population of the country.

As the period of nineteen months was too short to sterilize the whole people of this thickly populated country, the palace doctor set out immediately from the palace, for the Population Control Campaign, even without waiting for his first night with the royal bride. The poor Princess stayed in the palace-harem, dreaming about the manliness of the palace doctor and sleeping in utter uneasiness.

The palace doctor kept his nose to the grindstone and tried to bring the work conferred upon him to a complete success. First of all, he propagated the problems created by the population explosion as well as the inevitability of population control, throughout the country by sending palace-criers who announced them with the beating of their big-drums. But the people of this country who adored *'the male genital penetrated into the female genital,'* and who were quite aware of the great, eternal philosophy behind it, flatly ignored the words of the palace doctor. Thus, considering the great motto *'Talk less, work more,'* the palace doctor decided to organize sterilization camps throughout the country as well as to give incentives to the doctors who cooperated with the operation of the camps. But, to say with regret, things gradually moved towards a greater principle of compulsory sterilization, as nobody turned up voluntarily for this great act of patriotism.

At first, all the government employees were submitted to compulsory sterilization. Then, a law was implemented that each government employee should bring a minimum of one thousand persons to the sterilization camps or else they would lose their jobs. Those employees who brought more than one thousand persons to the camps were given immediate promotion and an attractive raise in their salary. In order to utilize this opportunity, all the employees formed themselves into violent gangs and such criminal bands, armed with fatal weapons, entered the houses where the people usually gathered in large numbers for a wedding or a funeral ceremony, and brought those poor souls to the sterilization camps, through seduction, criminal force or even assault. Bridegrooms were brought under compulsory sterilization, even without allowing them to spend their first night with their new brides, and one among them, even jumped into a well and committed suicide as he could not bear the grief and despair. Above all, a new law was passed that sterilization certificates should be presented for matters like getting treatment in government hospitals, buying food materials from ration shops, traveling in government vehicles, getting jobs in government departments and even for walking on National Highways!

By this time, needless to say, the sterilization camps all over the country were overflowing with members of the public. Even though first-aid materials were all used up, the sterilization continued in the usual tempo. The doctors who were tired of the twenty-four hour duty, handed over their work first to the nurses and then to the attendants and then, even to the barbers. But, when they too became tired of their work, certain carpenters and blacksmiths were appointed as *locum tenens* for doing the vasectomy operation. The carpenters carved the pubic-part of those who came for the operation and even sliced off their genitals with chisels. And the blacksmiths crushed the testicles of the patients by placing them on anvils and striking them with their hammers.

Those men who came to the hospitals for other treatments and those women, who came just for delivery, were put to sterilization even without their consent. The genital organs of all the children, born in hospitals, were removed in order to make them eunuchs.

The whole people of the country, whether male or female, young or old, were engaged in group-wailing and the whole nation was drowned in that heartbreaking cry. The frightening mass-cry of the emasculated and the unfeminined...! And when the sound of their wailing crossed the royal gates and reached the palace of the ruler, the notorious period of nineteen months was over...!

The palace doctor hurried to the palace-harem, expecting to lead a happy, conjugal life for the rest of his lifetime together with his wife, who had been living a virgin for all these nineteen months of her marriage. Later, as he was engaged in the art of love-making with his wife, he realized a fact that shocked him to the very core. Within the past term of nineteen months, his genital organ had been reduced to a very small one, just like that of new-born babe! His soul yearned for a sexual union with his wife, but his body was no more ready for it! As days and weeks passed one by one, he became disheartened and desperate. The Princess continued to soak her pillows with hot tears...

At last, recollecting her spirit and energy, the Princess invited the palace astrologer to her harem. The astrologer cast his cowries and whispered the only solution to the problem, in the ears of the Princess. According to the advice of the palace astrologer, the Princess had to give complete oil-massage to the best three stallions in the palace-stable, for ten consecutive days, beginning on the fifth day of her menstruation. While performing that rite, she should be completely naked and should cover her eyes; and the treatment had to be repeated for three consecutive moon-months. And thus, the Princess consulted the matter very secretly with the Palace-ostler and made every arrangement for the penance.

By the very next month of the visit of the royal astrologer, the Princess began to undergo the penance, systematically. All those ten days, the three stallions in the palace-stable neighed lustfully. They, sometimes, tried to mount the Princess but withdrew themselves without mating due to their bestial lack of intelligence. And the Palace-ostler stood silently in the stable watching the massage and enjoying the naked beauty of the blind-folded Princess.

The Palace-ostler became extremely lascivious as the days of the next moon-month approached. Thus, on the second moon-month, the ostler, who had exchanged a stallion for himself by covering his body with the hide of a horse, became the object of the Princess oil-massage! Though he behaved, at first like a horse before the Princess who too was passionate due to the heat of the horses, later, used the intelligence of a human being and mated with her. And on the third moon-month the Princess did not come to the palace-stable, as she had no menstruation!

The palace doctor, who was driven to despair by his impotency, was totally ignorant of the pregnancy of his wife.

So, one day, he decided to meet the palace-psychiatrist. The alienist discussed the symptoms, diagnosed the illness and suggested the treatment. He said that the disease came to the palace doctor just because he had been engaged in destroying the sexual potency of the male citizens of the country. He pointed out the history of the disease, linking it with Greek mythology, and said that even a son became impotent just because he had seen his father coming with blood-stained hands after castrating his rams!

The palace-psychiatrist suggested that the only treatment for the disease was the constant ceremonial worship of Siva-Lingam, the phallic emblem of the image of the erect penis, as a symbol of generative power, and the performance of its adoration rites! He also advised him to make pilgrimages to temples of Khajaraho, the sculptures of which would give back his sexual potency. When the palace doctor came back to the harem to convey this happy news to his wife, the Princess was reluctant to show even her face to him. The ladies-in-waiting at the palace-harem were asked to inform him that the Princess had been engaged in a special fast and meditation for getting the boon of a child!

Days and months crawled like years. One day, after a long tenure of Siva-lingam pooja in seclusion, the palace doctor was dressing up to meet the palace-psychiatrist, when the messengers came from the harem and informed him that the Princess had delivered a boy-child. As it was incredible news for him, he rushed to the harem in his chariot to find out the truth.

As the chariot was moving at its maximum speed, as if its wheels were not touching the ground, surprisingly enough the palace doctor became lustful and felt sexual potency. But, suddenly, he saw a vision in which the severed male-genitals began to fly around him, inside the chariot! Those bloodstained, blood-oozing and warm sex organs frightened him with a grotesque dance and threatened him by changing shapes and colors! Being gripped with fear, he shivered head to foot and jumped out of the running chariot. His head crashed on the ground and his genitals were crushed and severed under the chariot-wheel.

And the palace astrologer, drawing a diagram of the zodiac and casting his cowries, declared that the birth of a male-child on certain position of the planets in the constellations of stars would cause the death of either of its parents!

What a pity! Poor palace doctors who turn psychiatric 'cases' over night! Well, actually, it will be a surprise only if these foot-licking sycophants who create darkness by shutting their eyes and who do not distinguish the patient from the disease, are not turning into maniacs! And never will they be expiated!

The Wanderer felt strong disgust and indignation. He thought more and more about the palace doctor, the protagonist of the story narrated by the Erewhonian alienist. He restlessly rubbed his palms together and looked up vacantly with a sorrowful mien.

What a horrible mental disease! It is Ephiclus Complex, a psychiatric problem never mentioned in any books of Psychiatry! No doubt! If you go through the whole history of the world, you will come to understand that the king's son-in-law cum palace-doctor of Erewhon is the second person who ever suffered from such a mental disease. For, is it not clear that the first person is a Greek named Ephiclus!

The Wanderer gave a push to the stone on which the biography of the Erewhonian palace-doctor was inscribed, and it rolled down to the base of the valley.

Let that stone roll and roll, and fall on the wide bosom of the Ganges! Let all the rulers and the ruled of the whole world come to know and be prepared for the horrible recurring of such a terrible mental disease! For it is highly necessary that all the citizens who love their country must know about it.

But what is there in simply blaming the sculptors, the doctors and the guards of the palace? History proves that even selfish, power-seeking kings and queens also become mental patients! And the condition of the artists under them is too pathetic! Is the history of the First Queen of China itself not a sufficient example? But, in that case too, how far can we believe the fidelity of the historians?

Almost all the historians have described in detail the first queen of China. But every one of them had conveniently kept as top secret certain ugly events that occurred during the benevolent despotism of that great queen.

For the same reason itself, it is simply the duty of a patriotic citizen to write down those matters for the scholars who are interested in doing research work in History.

The Wanderer selected a big stone. His heart was throbbing

in gratitude to Pearl S. Buck who wrote in detail about the last empress of China. And then, he began to peck on the stone assiduously, certain hidden facts concerning the first empress of China...

Almost all the historians have pointed out that though the first queen of China was not herself an artist, she had lavishly promoted arts and encouraged the artists. But none of them has noted down the historical truth that she had encouraged only those eunuchs and those who had consented to become eunuchs, who had been experts in the art of painting, sculpture, music and literature, and that all other artists had been sent to the prisons. And that is why, in this brief addendum-note on history, emphasis is given only to the queen and to the artists who lived during her reign.

The father of the queen was not only an artist himself but also a promoter of all the artists in the country and had never shown any distinction between the eunuchs and others. The only mistake he committed was that he had entrusted his only heir to the throne under the protection of certain faithful eunuchs, as he had no time to look after her during those busy days of administration and diplomacy.

But, in the passage of time, the princess invited a palace servant into her bedroom, without the knowledge of the king or her guards, and both of them lived for sometime as husband and wife. The king, who was quite a rationalist, at first, con-sidered this a personal affair of the princess, as a mere matter of fun or a sort of biological necessity. But, he began to look at it very seriously when the princess gave birth to her second son. In fact, his heart was full of appreciation for the princess as she had *brought forth men-children only* to rule the country after her death.

Later, the king became sleepless, thinking how he could hand over the rein of the kingdom to his irresponsible daughter who was spending her days and nights engaged in the game of love and lust with a palace-servant, without caring for learning administrative matters. At last, according to the advice of the chief eunuch, the king ordered to cut off the head of that palace-servant, and thus, relieved his successor to the throne from the octopus-grip of conjugal life. Having regained her equanimity from the bereavement of her mate's death, the princess not only began to show interest in the administration of the kingdom, but, when her father died, enthroned herself as the First Queen of China.

And this brief history ought to be written only on the artists who had lived during the golden reign of the queen! Among those artists, the most notable painter was a eunuch named Fessan Huiem, who was pretty famous all over China. He had begun his career as a street painter but gradually acquired mastery in weird painting. In one of his major paintings, he had even depicted the queen in the shape of China. He had drawn the picture of the queen inside the boundary line of the map of China and thus had given the profile of the queen to China. Moreover, the picture was drawn in such a way that it seemed, as it was equally divided into two parts, that the queen with one side of her face was blessing her friends with a benign smile and with the other side was threatening her enemies with a frightful look. No wonder, the queen offered him a number of awards and rewards in cash and kind.

All the artists of the country who were eunuchs competed with each other in pleasing the queen. Poets and other writers of literature wrote poems and other forms of literature praising the queen. Famous groups of singers in the country stood at all important junctions and sat by the side of busy streets and sang psalms and hymns glorifying the queen. The traveling storytellers wandered from one end to the other end of the country, spreading mysterious stories about the magical powers of the queen. The sculptors carved and pecked the words and verses of the queen on red stones and white stones, and installed or erected them throughout the country. And the queen sent all the artists who were not ready to praise her and her reign to the prisons and even banned the exhibition of their masterpieces in the art galleries of the country.

The majority of the people not only worshipped her but also blindly believed that she was an incarnation of some divine being. While men accepted her as their dream-girl, young women took her up as a model. The strangest thing was that even the grand-old men and grand-old women considered the young queen to be their mother!

Though things were like this, a few among the subjects made unnecessary harangues and timely pulpit sermons on the queen's past history and her life with the palace-servant. To those who objected to such accusations, they pointed to the two sons of the queen as evidence.

However, the majority of the people who blindly adored the queen could not believe the purely personal events in her past. They had already drowned those old stories in the depth of oblivion. Moreover, it was beyond their power of imagination that their queen had lain with an ordinary palace-servant, had been impregnated with his ordinary semen and had delivered two ordinary children! Though there was the clear evidence of two princes, most of them ignored them and tried to convince others that the queen had given birth to them through her ears! Many of them believed it as the history of the country itself was based on legends and epics! Above all, they spread a false idea that the two princes had some divine power in them as they were born with golden spoons in their mouths.

Though some other matters were casually scribbled, this brief history is solely on the artists who had lived during the reign of the First Queen of China. As the queen was ageing, the eunuch-artists became highly enthusiastic. The Chinese poets of the period secretly composed elegies and poetic lamentations in order to be sung immediately after the queen's death, and great musicians of China gave tune and music to them. Painters drew the queen's pictures in her different poses and various facial expressions. Among the members of the public who were unable to believe that their queen would one day become old or she would die, the pictures of her youthful days were in great demand. Artists showed their expertise by giving rose-colored bony cheeks, dark deer-like eyes as well as red-hued wet lips to the queen.

Sculptors and statue-makers very confidently made full-size statues and busts of the queen in order to be erected at every junction, when she died. Almost all the artists took great care to project the feminine beauty of the queen in all their statues and paintings. While making even the busts of the queen, those sculptors competed with each other in increasing the measurement of her chest!

Each artist painted the queen as Mother, Sister, Wife or Daughter in accordance with his imagination. Poets described her, kudos to their fancy, either as the goddess who keeps friends close to her bosom or as the demon that kills with a roar all the enemies, or as the fertile soil that gives good harvest, or as the wine that intoxicates the youth, or as the nutritious milk with which children are nurtured. To sum up, that era *in toto* was filled with a sort of queen-ism. Almost all the artists, and even the so-called intelligentsia, who lived during the reign of the First Queen of China, had changed themselves into eunuchs and, in such a situation, there is nothing to be surprised at this syndrome!

"**F**or there are some eunuchs, which were so born from their mother's womb: and there are some eunuchs, which were made eunuchs of men: and there be eunuchs, which have made themselves eunuchs for the kingdom..." How rightly Jesus classified them!

The Wanderer despondently realized the fact that if he had continued to inscribe all about those artists and litterateurs who were eunuchs by birth, or transformed into eunuchs by others or self-made eunuchs, there would be no use save the breaking of the tip of his chisel!

These frigid people, whose body, mind and soul are frozen, whose thinking brain and feeling heart are benumbed, may be appointed as the guards of their rulers' bedrooms! They are only capable of carrying out such duties! For they could never bring out the bedroom secrets of their kings and queens! They are just like marble statues!

But the saddest part of it is that the slow-witted and imbecile subjects are too unscrupulous to respect and adore these gigolos! Isn't the brief autobiography of that Erewhonian Guard an apt illustration for it? Though some-what obscure like a fairytale, is it not sufficient to disclose the idiocy of the people?

The Wanderer concentrated his mettle and resumed his inscribing, selecting a new piece of granite...

Ours was a vast country of teeming millions. Being blessed by natural beauty and enriched by food crops and cash crops, our country attracted many foreigners from time immemorial. As a result, not only a number of foreign kings and militarists but also barbarians and even merchants, many a time attacked and conquered our country. But then we, the people, never cared for or even thought about the joy and pleasure of ruling the country for ourselves!

As time passed likewise, a person, who had been settled in our country, one day became self-conscious of the joy and pleasure of ruling the country and cultivated conscientiousness among us. Though we never believed in such talks, his handsome nature and his oratory attracted and united us. As his charisma had enslaved us and as there was little time to find another suitable person, our elders decided to anoint him as our own king. And thus, thenceforth, a mere superstition that 'we ourselves rule our country' spread among the people.

Under the autocratic rule of our king, the subjects passed their days, eating and sleeping, giving and receiving in marriage, begetting children and simply dying, just as they did in the past. After a few years, our king died suddenly and we anointed his only daughter for that vacant throne. For the beauty of the princess had that much mesmeric effect on us that, needless to say, we became mere slaves under her spell of beauty.

Though the late king was a staunch supporter of autocracy, our country slithered down to democracy as and when the queen took over the reins of administration. There was a deep-rooted belief among the people that woman by birth is non-reliant and that she gains her perfection only with the man, and this superstition might be the reason that made our queen a supporter of democracy. Moreover, the queen personally desired the constant presence of a man with her. And, that was how the queen promoted seven of us, including myself, as her ministers and made us her chamberlains, or rather her personal guards. And, even in our country 'seven' was considered always a lucky number!

And the queen, who always respected the system of democracy, gave us the rank and position of 'the husband' strictly according to our seniority. In fact, that was a tradition we got from our great epic poems. Thus the senior most among us, or the First Man, became the husband of the queen. Though we, the other ministers, were naturally jealous of the fortune of the First Man, we never showed any reluctance in delivering our duty as the guards of the queen's bed chamber, for we were quite optimistic and happy that one day each one of us would also get the same lucky chance. Even in the great epic *Maha Bharata,* the heroine *Panchali* had five husbands, and of course, we loved and followed the ways of such great heroes and heroines of the past.

As the days passed one by one, the queen became more and more healthy and beautiful. And we furtively rejoiced at heart, seeing the First Man turning weary and old, his health and vitality waning day by day. One day, it happened just as we had expected. Our queen saved democracy and honored our country by deposing the First Man from the rank and position of the husband and promoting the Second Man to that covetable post.

The horrible fate of the First Man repeated in the case of the Second Man and in the Third Man as well. And I, the Seventh Man, being drowned in sweet dreams, patiently waited for the day on which I would become the husband of the queen, and guarded the bed chamber of the queen without any grumbling. And those old and weary ministers, who were the former husbands of the queen, consoled themselves by heaving hot sighs and derived vicarious satisfaction by peeping through the keyhole into the queen's bedroom. As usual, the Sixth Man also became weary and old and I, the Seventh and Last Man in the queen's cabinet, was promoted to the rank and position of the queen's husband.

On the first night, myself, who entered the bed chamber of the queen, became highly passionate and lustful, thinking of the moment in which my long cherished desire to be consummated. Naturally, the queen began to take up the administrative matters with me systematically. But, soon, the queen began panting heavily and heaving long sighs. Lying quite exhausted, she started sobbing and lamenting in a whisper, "Ha! What has become of me? Oh God! What really has happened to me?"

For a moment, being shocked by discontent, grief and despair, I stood there like a stone-statue. Gradually, I began to realize the horrible change that occurred to the queen due to my presence, and the frightful consequences that would come to our country in the near future.

I silently watched how the abilities of the queen suddenly faded away and turned futile just before my own physical strength and willpower. Though I felt pity and fear at the changes that had come to the queen, soon after my taking up the office of the queen's husband, I was quite aware of the obligations of a husband, and pushed away the days in anguish and despair. Later, though outwardly the queen appeared to be beautiful with the magic taught secretly by her father, only I knew the exact truth that she had already become too old, physically and mentally.

I was not surprised when the queen, who had lost her femininity, became an autocrat just like her father. There onwards, almost all the decisions taken by the queen were too cruel. First of all, she, with her mysterious charm, transformed all the six erstwhile husbands into marble statues. Then, she, in the name of equality, began to destroy the femininity and masculinity of the people, obviously to make them weak like her, both in mental and physical matters. These kinds of activities of the queen heightened the fear and anxiety of the people, and they turned their attention to appropriate revolutionary means. However, I alone pushed away my days like a Laodicean, due to my sincere love for the queen, silently discharging my duties as the guard of her bed chamber.

The non-aphrodisiac measures of the queen turned to be the straw that broke the camel's back. The masses had become furious enough to upturn the whole country. The elders of the people, together with those who were cherishing the dream of becoming future kings, queens or guards, gave leadership to the people's insurrection. The rioters and the mutineers captured most of the places and, at last, approached the palace slowly and steadily. It was at that moment that the queen, who did not know what to do, fell down at my feet, and sobbed and wailed in utter despair and agony. I shared her sorrow and consoled her, just like any other husband would do if such a critical situation had come to him, still keeping the sanctity of the rank and position conferred upon me. Later, I told her the only way to escape from the mounting danger and she readily agreed to it.

In accordance with our common decision, soon, an enclosed tomb was constructed inside the palace itself. Then, a beautiful life-like marble-statue of the queen was hurriedly made and laid on the top of the grave. At a glimpse, it appeared as if the queen were taking her eternal rest on the upper platform of the tomb. But, on lifting the statue, there could be seen a secret entrance to go into the dark cellar of the grave.

I brought the marble-statues of the six erstwhile husbands of the queen and positioned them as guards to the queen's marble statue. They were placed on both sides of the statue, two at the feet, two at the waist and two at the head. Then I personally went to the bed chamber of the queen and led her to the tomb. I lifted the statue and sent the queen down to the cellar through the secret entrance. Once I found her ensconced in the grave, I closed the secret door and re-positioned the marble statue at the top of the grave. And then, I sat at the head of the queen's statue and began shedding tears and lamenting repeatedly in a loud voice, "Our queen is dead. Alas! Our queen is dead, long live the queen."

Suddenly, the rioters and the mutineers captured the palace and its premises, and enthroned their leader as the next king. After that, the people came one by one to the tomb, and prostrated themselves before the queen as well as her erstwhile guards, wailing in great distress and sorrow at the passing away of their queen. Then, they returned home with great peace, consolation and happiness, their faces beaming with high satisfaction. Our people used to give great respect for the dead male and for the dead or living female, ignoring their crimes and pardoning their sins.

As I was looking at the splendid marble statue of the queen, I felt suddenly as if I gained some spiritual fulfillment or enlightenment. I was seeing just before my eyes, as if in a reverie, the real queen who had been my sole hope and who would have become the perfect satisfaction of my life and for whom I had waited a man's span of life. And while I was gaining tremendous bliss by staring at the charming body of the queen's marble-statue, and running both my hands on her lovely face and caressing her lips and cheeks, the real queen who by this time had become physically and mentally old was dying from suffocation, without getting oxygen in the dark cellar of the grave!

As days passed, a cold crept up my legs and hands and I felt my body benumbed. One day, I discovered the shocking truth that I too was gradually being transformed into a marble statue, from foot to head. However, just before my eyes and ears turned into marble, I saw what I had to see and I heard what I had to hear.

The people of our country constantly pass by the royal tomb in the palace. One by one, they come to the front of the tomb in a solemn procession with folded arms in obeisance and kowtow before it. They are whispering in a tone of adoration:

"Most Holy Queen and the Seven August Guards,
We most humbly adore you,
For you became marble statues for our cause,
And with all our hearts render you,
The Homage due to your Sovereign Majesty. Amen."

*Hail! Salam! Namaste! Vanakkam!*

Various forms of obeisance! Kudos not only to the

kings and queens but also to their guards! Bow to the marble-turned gigolos even!

The Wanderer's heart fumed with fury. His whole body churned in a whirl of anger. Tears of wrath blistered his cheeks!

Even without an insurrection of the people, queens may turn into marble statues! History will repeat! Don't you hear the lamentation of a queen whose nose changed the course of history?

> *I have nothing*
> *Of woman in me: now from head to foot*
> *I am marble - constant...*

But what's happening here! Hailing the statues just after a successful revolution! Or, leading a successful revolution, just for the sake of bowing before the statues! What a shameful situation!

You, Youngsters! How can you suffer this slavery? Or how long? Do you think that your blood and water, your flesh and marrow, are only for erecting pyramids for your kings and queens? Don't you feel your brain rusting inside your skulls?

For a moment a sort of enthusiasm and zeal waved in the heart of the Wanderer. Then, like a burnt-down pyre, his mind became pacific.

Who shall be blamed for this situation? Here, even intelligent and imaginative youngsters too are helpless! Nobody is here to guide them! They request and plead for help! But, it becomes too late when they find out that those who offer guidance to them are deceivers! What a pitiable situation!

Is it not such a story that a young Erewhonian told me, while roaming through the streets of Erewhon?

On a new block of granite, the Wanderer began to inscribe, in that Erewhonian's own language, the story of their hopes and blasted hopes, the epic of their brave struggles...

We are educated youngsters who, having been ignored by the elite group, live outside the citadel, but we have the clear-cut knowledge of rules and regulations of the rulers and the governments as well as of the much appraised mottoes of equality, fraternity and liberty. Because there is not a single day in which Marx, Mao and Che Guevara do not come for discussion into our huts where kerosene lamps flicker gloomily and dimly. That does not mean that we are all rebels or revolutionaries! Is it not because of the fact that we, who study much, understand more than what we study and think about much more than what we understand, differ fundamentally in our natures that the commanders of the citadel could suppress us with their 'divide and rule' policy?

Generally speaking, we are all youngsters - brave, enthusiastic and idealistic. And don't misunderstand that we are all mere dreamers just because we usually think over economic equality, liberation theology, freedom-based world peace and production based distribution.

We won't say that there are no 'up-lookers' among us. They often compare the socio-economic-political system which we plan to establish with the Christians' Kingdom of God or with the Hindus' *'Ramarajya'* the Kingdom of Ram. Or, at times, like indolent creatures, they chant Plato's Republic or More's Utopia.

There are a few 'in-lookers' too among us. They push on their lives, by giving themselves completely into the hands of fate, and by welcoming all the right-less duties. They surrender their own ideals to get the friendship of others as well as to escape from the tragic realities of life imposed on them by the environment, and they live their lives opportunistically like the willow trees that toss their heads left and right when the storm blows and stand erect as it subsides.

Besides, there are a few 'back-lookers' and a few 'front-lookers' among us. The back-lookers try to evaluate the existing circumstances and to justify their laziness by interpreting history. Meanwhile, the front-lookers, being fully conscious of the prosperity prevailing in other countries, do many things hurriedly and thoughtlessly like moonstruck persons, and later, being exhausted of their energy like the fire-obsessed termite-flies, sit *tiredly* on the graves of their own miscalculations!

We know that there is no special benefit in blaming all these groups together or separately as we are all equally aggrieved of residing outside the citadel. And between us and the executives who rule us, there is this long and high, un-climbable and invincible, wall that protects the caucus. On the other side of the fortress, the commanders who rule us, enjoy their life by cracking jokes and quarrelling with each other to pass their time and, at times, by throwing breadcrumbs towards us over the fortress to distract our attention.

How could we, the young and the literate, tolerate such an

injustice? Most of us simply concentrate our attention on accumulating or on distributing the breadcrumbs that fall from the other side of the great wall! When the psychological differences created by ourselves by studying ideals and their various interpretations as well as the physical differences created in us automatically by the variations in the availability of the breadcrumbs which were thrown to us, amalgamated each other, some of us even began to fear that the new earth of our dreams would turn to be a mere illusion! And that is how we came to the decision of climbing over the great wall and establishing the new world by ousting the present rulers through fair or foul methods.

It was quite unexpectedly that we met and acquainted ourselves with monitor lizards, while walking around the fort in search of some easy access into the citadel. In great amazement, we watched these monitor lizards who climbed up and down so effortlessly on the smooth sides and surface of the great wall and, thereby, simultaneously established good relationships with the extraordinary commanders on the other side of the wall as well as with the ordinary folks, including us, on this side of the wall. As there was no other way to enter the fort, we made a treaty with them. According to that treaty, the monitor lizards agreed to make conciliatory talks with the commanders of the citadel as well as to carry us over to the other side of the fort by using their heads or tails.

And we hopefully waited. At last, the monitor lizards informed us with great joy that their mediatory talks with the commanders were highly successful. According to the consensus reached, all of us had either to wear white gowns or cover our body with saffron clothes or tonsure our heads or wear turbans or caps on our heads. Some of us who agreed to these conditions were allowed to enter the citadel through the main gate, and the commanders appointed them to organize carnivals for their pleasure and to issue license for their lechery.

We waited and waited patiently. The monitor lizards, who returned after a second round of talks with the commanders, came to us with a smile of victory. They informed us that according to the conditions of the new consensus, we had to wear either olive-green or khaki colored clothes! Those among us who agreed to these clauses were allowed to enter into the citadel through the main gate, and the commanders appointed those who were dressed in khaki as their security men and those who were dressed in olive-green as the sentinels of the citadel!

Yet, a few people like us were left behind on this side of the citadel, as we were not ready to accept their conditions or clauses and we had already declared that the entrance into the citadel was a birthright beyond all conditions. So, we secretly decided to climb over the wall through whatsoever means or even by hanging on the tails of the monitor lizards, as there was no other way. And the monitors gladly fell in with our resolution.

Then onwards, we gripped at the tails of the monitor lizards and they pulled us up to the top of the wall. But, before we could reach the top of the wall, they shook us off from their tails. And while we were lying down with our broken hands and legs and backbones, they crawled down towards us as if sympathizing with our fate and encouraged us to hold more tightly at their tails and even they laughed at us pointing out that we did not know how to hang on their tails properly. Those among us whose backbones were not yet broken believed their words and attempted again and again to climb over the wall, hanging on their tails. And the monitor lizards were finally successful in shaking us off their tails till one and all of us broke our backbones.

It was too late when we realized the true color of these monitor lizards. At present, we the youngsters, being deprived of our backbones, are in the efforts of molding up a new generation of educated youth. And we are waiting for that remarkable day on which they will crush down the citadel, oust the rulers by frightening them to the core and establish the good earth of our dreams; we are waiting, and waiting patiently...

Try! And try again and again! Be optimistic!

Only constant effort and sacrifice will lead you to the final emancipation. One day, a dawn of equality and liberty will blossom! And let us wait patiently for that wonderful 'tomorrow'.

The knell for these disguised and deceitful public-servants and press-barons has already been ringing in the air. Hey, Youngsters! The day of extinction of the monitor lizards, which were cheating you all these days, is also fast-approaching! Like bats, they stand this minute with birds, showing their wings, and the next with beasts, displaying their teeth! Like eels, they stand with the snake by thrusting out their heads, and with the fish by waving their tails! These wobblers are the real deceivers and they must be included in the hit-list as public enemies of the first order!

The time is over for the pulling-down of these black citadels! The cruel commander of the citadel has already been haunted by fear! Oh, Erewhonian! You know what happens in the citadel! Say aloud your own experience in the citadel! Just open your heart and shout!

There is nothing for you to fear! Fear is the monopoly of those who keep and care for power! You have nothing to lose but your chains! You realize these truths and so, oh Erewhonian, cry out in your loudest voice what you see and experience in that black citadel!

The Wanderer felt as if the waves of an oration reached his eardrums. He took his chisel and began to peck on a new piece of rock... the witnessing of an Erewhonian...

I, who was leading a calm and quiet life in this citadel, so suddenly, like a bolt out of the clear blue, realized that truth at last! Even without sitting under the shade of a banyan tree, I came across the enlightenment that 'power fears always'. Fear like the sword of Damocles, dangles on a single hair and swings to and fro over the head of the rulers! But the pleasure given by that throne or chair of power urges man to clutch onto it. Look! How foolish or senseless it is!

Is it only Man who becomes a prey to fear? Even God, from time immemorial, is being gripped by fear! What God had done to Lucifer and his followers who questioned His power and who were a threat to His throne, is quite familiar like a folktale to all of us, isn't it? Just try to imagine the arrogant face of God who sits impudently on the throne in heaven, after pushing them down into the fire-pit of Hell! Don't you feel nauseated when you look at that visage of God, who for the sake of power and glory had to adopt the cruelest and mean method to suppress a group of angels who were ardent believers of democracy?

Don't be excited! Well! These people know how to sail sitting on two boats! They are ardent believers of democracy and of kingship, whether of man or of God, at the same time! Forget it!

As I am wandering inside this citadel, I cannot even single out God alone and accuse Him! Even our invaluable epics present the history of gods and goddesses, whose total number outnumbers the total number of the whole human beings, who destroyed all those who questioned their power and sovereignty, using the dirtiest and the foulest tricks!

Meanwhile, I accept to a certain extent the historical truth that power is divine. But how sad it is when we, from antiquity, foolishly believe and blindly accept that there is divinity even in all the cruelties applied by periodical rulers to retain their power and supremacy!

Is it meant that no one shall be anxious or shall worry about the present critical situation and unfortunate plight of this citadel? Never! My humble wish is that we must realize the truth and shall not be mere cowards.

Let me make it pretty clear. Aren't we witnessing for years how those who occupy the Chair of Power just by chance, use the so-called 'divine cruelty' for retaining their power and even implement it through their soldiers and followers? And that is the reason why I could face the cruelty prevailing inside the citadel with equanimity and self-control. In order to describe in detail the cruelties imposed by the commander of the citadel, can I neither think over them properly nor recollect them systematically. I stammer and stutter in my search for apt words!

The present sad situation existing in this citadel as well as the cruel means adopted by the commander of this fort to retain his power lead me towards certain historical truths. In fact, the rulers dare to take up cruel means only for two reasons. The first one is that the rulers, urged by their avidity to extend power, ruin and destroy those who are outside the limits of their judicial boundary. The second one is that the rulers, due to their fear of losing power, ruin and destroy those who are living under his sole jurisdiction. But, I see a sum total of both these cruelties inside this citadel.

How tragic is this sight! Here, the commander, realizing the fact that his own Chair of Power slips away from him in his attempts to extend power beyond his judicial boundary, tries to overcome fear through cold-blooded assassination of his own subjects, and suppressing rather effeminizing them, physically and mentally.

In ancient days, kings and militarists had directly planned and implemented these types of cruelties. But what really is the present situation inside this fortress? Owing to the increase in population, the commander himself prepares a scheme of cruelties and implements it simply through his own faithful soldiers! Now, we can well imagine how careful is the commander of this fort in appointing all the available sadists and scoundrels in the country as his soldiers!

Why should I accuse the commander of the citadel alone? Are we not seeing quite often how inside this fort the followers of the commander quarrel among themselves, or different groups of laymen fight with each other for establishing the power and position of a particular individual or of a typical group through the designing and implementation of cruelties? Is it not a common phenomenon inside the citadel that various gangs argue and fight among themselves to establish or retain the supremacy of a particular gang or group, by crushing and destroying other gangs or groups through wicked means of dire cruelty? Such fights and self-assertive arguments are quite common among the theistic groups that practice different customary rites, among the atheistic groups that believe in different rationalistic formulae, among the political groups that zealously stick to different ideologies and even among the social groups that dream of different goals. Thus, how many of these human-worms have been crucified or burnt alive or even become food for the edge of swords! And simply because of these facts, I must become fully conscious of the condition of this citadel.

Soon, I realized the truth that the commander of the fort alone knew the value of femininity and masculinity. Moreover, almost all the soldiers of the commander were eunuchs and, so, inside the citadel they carried out their master's cruelties without caring whether their victims were male or female citizens. The implementation of the commander's atrocities was not very difficult for the soldiers as the people inside the citadel, being devoid of sufficient food or clothing, were sighing, and sobbing, and cursing their fate, over their immediate basic requirements. While the wails and cries of the naked and half-naked men and women were melting the black stones of the citadel, the ruler was moving towards victory as he had succeeded in plugging the ears of his soldiers with pulp!

Another truth was that the roaring laughter of the soldiers could easily drown the ear-breaking cries of the frightened masses! Perhaps, you are wondering how those who belong to the species of Man or who have been born as human beings could implement such horrible and frightful cruelties! But don't be shocked when I reveal a few such gruesome incidents!

First of all, the soldiers of the commander, roamed along the streets, crashed into the houses by midnight, caught whoever was available there and transported them to jails.

They were following the old edict of Machiavelli: For injuries ought to be done all at one time, so that being tasted less, they offend less!

Once the jails were filled with innocent subjects, the murderous maniacs began their brutish experiments on the victims. The soldiers with their pries tore apart the muscles of the strong, half-naked men! They pierced the breasts of beautiful, half-naked women with red-hot needles and, at times, even established their rights over them by branding their backs and buttocks with hot iron-seals on which the first letters of the brander concerned were inscribed!

Even the utmost cruelty itself will be ashamed if it comes to know of the ineffable facts of this citadel! Pins crawled under the fingernails of children! The flesh of young men disjointed from their bones under the rub-down of pole-pestles made from the trunk of aged coconut trees, and even the testicles of some of them were bruised and crushed in that notorious process of the so-called retribution. Many of them were bastinadoed to admit the crimes of which they were unaware. Tailors were appointed to drive needles under their fingernails, and clothespins into their nipples and genitals, and feathers into their ears and nostrils! Thrusting needles into the teats of young maidens, they squeezed blood out of their tender breasts. Old men and old women were buried under the mounts of nails pulled away from the fingers of those innocent victims! While heated, raw coconut-needles were thrust up through the urinary opening of penises to the very source of semen, bamboo batons penetrated the wombs of virgins and violated the chastity of married women.

Youngsters were put in dark dungeons and torture chambers for their only crime of believing in equality, fraternity and liberty! They waited for their turn to be brainwashed either through shock therapy or drug therapy, so that their mind would become a clean slate, 'a writing tablet on which as yet nothing actually stands written,' as Aristotle said. There, instead of the old slogans, they tried to engrave new slogans like inequality, hostility and suppression or slavery as mottos of human existence! Thus, the prediction of Prophet Orwell was fulfilled: We shall squeeze you empty, and then we shall fill you with ourselves.

The intelligentsia of the citadel, who shouted under Victorious-light, was taken to the hospital for drug therapy. Overdoses of insulin were injected into their veins and drugs like nitrous oxide, chlorpromazine, melicon, largactil, sodium amytal and thorazine were forcibly served to lower their intellectual efficiency and, then, to bring a slow death by damaging their internal organs. Anti-sleeping tablets like dexytrine were given so that they could not sleep for weeks! Many of them were given high voltage electroshocks through electric metal beds, dragon chairs and cattle prods in order to blast back the victims into their infancy!

No! Can any human being imagine the ubiquitous techniques used by the brutish soldiers of the citadel? Or can anyone with a human heart describe the horrible spectacles of this citadel? But, Oh, Commander! How long can you direct these cruelties? Oh, Soldiers! How long can you implement these cruelties? Oh, Citizens! How long can you suffer and tolerate these cruelties?

Oh, soldiers with closed ears, if you think that the wailing and the weeping of the people are powerless or useless, you are living in a fool's paradise! Haven't you learnt the story of the Jericho Walls that fell down at the voice of the people? By now itself, some of the stones of this citadel have started melting down in the weeping and crying of the people! There is not much time left for the commander's Chair of Power to flow away in the flood of people's tears!

Though helpless, I am waiting in full optimism. For, things that must happen will happen at the ripeness of time! 'Keiy sera sera' as the Spanish people say! Can the cruelty of the commander or the weeping of the people or even the hardness of the stones with which this very same citadel has been built up, change the already destined course of Fate? Can it...?

**Y**es! It can! It can be...!

No need for doubting! But, first of all, one must know what that fate is!

Fate will be a curse for those who think that their laziness, or their lack of intelligence, or their indifference, or their placidity, is fate! And all the rest will gain their salvation! When righteous men are crucified, it marks the birth of a new age! How long one can hide this historical truth? Aren't you seeing that the scriptures and the prophecies in them are fulfilled to their very letters? Aren't you hearing how those parents who have lost their children beat on their breasts and weep?

> *In Rama was there a voice heard, lamentation,*
> *and weeping and great mourning,*
> *Rachel weeping for her children...*

Where are those children? Perhaps they are dying, inch by inch, suffering the cruel tortures of the soldiers! Perhaps the soldiers might have destroyed their dead bodies without leaving a single bone to trace as evidence of their erstwhile existence! Perhaps their carcasses are taken to the jungle and burnt to ashes, by pouring petrol over them!

The Wanderer's face reddened with emotions. Tears flowed out of his eyes, spontaneously. Into some deep thought, he drowned, his fingers dug into his rough beard. And there in the firmament, clouds began marking the forehead of Kang-chenzdonga with vermilion!

At times, scriptures are fulfilled just literally. At other times, they are fulfilled with slight deviations. Instead of hanging the Sons of Man on crosses, they may be hanged on the lintels of doors and bars of windows! If it happens so, the emendation in scriptures may be like this:

"They beat me with their batons. They broke my bones, one by one. They pierced my heart even without spearing me with their lances."

To be crucified for committing no crimes! To be asked to confess to an unstated crime, and to be penalized just to clear or write off a case! To be compelled to go to the offices of law and order, till friends and relatives become suspicious, till you yourself feel a general sense of guilt! At last, to be mentally prepared to receive any cruel verdict for an uncommitted crime! Alas! How hopeless is the fate of *Franz Kafka's* Joseph K. and other citizens like him!

Where is that Golgotha? Where is the righteous being crucified? Didn't I hear that gospel somewhere in Erewhon? Let it also become a part of history, marking the beginning of a great change!

The Wanderer brandished his chisel and began to peck on a new piece of granite...

As he had fallen down completely exhausted by their cruel torture, they made him stand erect and bound his legs and hands tightly to the bars of the window. They gagged and scourged him. They undressed him and thrust his own loincloth into his mouth so that he could not even utter his last sacred verses!

The soldiers who came prowling in the loneliness of midnight, firstly, cordoned off his house preventing the escape of even a housefly. Then they broke the doors with a blast and rushed into the house like unexpected mountain torrents! Before getting a chance to know what was happening, they pinioned him, who was the only male in the family, the sire and supporter of the home, against the bars of the window.

Before the reverence, or rather the surprise, aroused in the mind by the color of the soldier's uniform, left their hearts; all the women of the family were brought before him and were made to stand in a row against the wall!

As he stood against the window with straining ears and staring eyes, his heart, then, was splitting in utter helplessness and hopeless bondage! A rare fate under which one could feel no senses but seeing and hearing!

His eight-year-old daughter cried aloud as if she was seeing before her the devils of her great-grandma's tales about ghosts! His sister, who was standing on the threshold of marriage, tried to suppress her cries in the height of her exasperation. His wife was pleading in her vaulting helplessness. His mother, who had painfully given birth to him, wept and wailed pulling out her hair and beating on her breasts. His grandmother, who had been straining her ears for the death bell, cursed her fate and grinned with a ghastly smile.

Yielding to despair, he stood there under the shower of ear-breaking vituperations from the soldiers! He heard the drunken soldiers roaring in their voluptuousness, their inebriating eyes scaling up and down the female creatures that were standing in a row against the wall: So! You are the revolutionaries, eh? Well! Strip off, everybody! And be quick. Let's see where you have hidden the hand-bombs and wooden-spears!

One of those brutes, pinching at the tiny nipples of his little daughter who was trembling with fear, shouted, "Oh, these are mere small crackers! In future, these too will develop into grenades!" And with a devilish laugh, he hurled the child out of the room.

"These are mere useless bombs which passed the expiry date!" exclaimed another soldier, pulling hard at the wrinkled breasts of the grandmother. He caught that old woman by the neck and pushed her into the darkness of the courtyard.

He, who was the sire and head of the family, closed his eyes tightly, as the soldiers removed all the clothes of his own mother. While a soldier was hitting in between her thighs with his baton, the Centurion standing impatiently outside the house, called out, "Boys! Have you searched every nook and corner? Did you find any dangerous weapon?"

"Yes, Sir! We are searching for spears, Sir!" one soldier shouted back. With a new spirit, he came towards the head of the family and stamped at the helpless man's groin with his horseshoed-boot. The poor, just and innocent man howled in severe pain. The soldier with a satisfied face looked out of the room and said, "Sir! I have just broken one spear with my boot,

Sir! And all the rest are hand-bombs, Sir!'

Another soldier caught hold of his mother's hair and pushed her towards the Centurion. The bound-up family-head, heard him shouting, "Sir! Take her into custody. Her weapons are not so bad, Sir!"

The helpless family-head, for a moment, saw his dearest wife and his only sister, who were made naked by the soldiers, sitting in a corner of the room, trembling with fear. He raised his eyes upwards and they seemed to be entangled somewhere in vacuity.

Another soldier bruised his wife's uncovered breasts with his nails, and he heard the brute growl, "Are these bombs explosive?" Then, with one end of his baton, he hit below her abdomen and commented, "Got it! This is the place where you used to keep his spear, isn't it?"

That so-called protector of law caught her by the hair and pushed her towards a wooden cot. His own wife's heart-breaking voice resounded in the ears of the family-head, "No! Alas! Please, don't...! Kill me, if you want! But don't..."

Squeezing the breasts of his marriageable sister, another soldier was shouting, "Give me a few seconds, I shall blunt the points of these spikes; otherwise, they will pierce and wound my chest!" She wriggled in pain as that beast was biting at the teats of her virgin-breasts!

Under the iron-grip of his strong hands, she writhed and trembled. He pushed her to the floor and made her lie on her back. He tickled in her private parts and interrogated, "Where, you bitch, is your deadly weapon?"

The poor wretch stammered, sobbing and panting, "Alas! Don't kill me, please! Believe me! Never in my life have I seen a hand-bomb or a wooden-spear!"

"Ah! Ha! Poor girl! I shall show them, now itself! Every other matter is secondary!" He bellowed like a wild animal and loosened the buttons of his pants.

In a flash, the head of the family saw the face of his eight-year-old daughter that was stained by her scalding tears. Her eyes were burning wrathfully in the dim light of the room. She was prowling towards that soldier who was raping her aunt and in her raised hand he saw a glittering kitchen-knife!

The head of the family, who was bound to the bars of the window, felt tiredness crawling up his body. Then, he raised his head and stared at some secret entrance to heaven. His mind was screaming in utter helplessness, *"Father, forgive them; for they know not what they do."*

He began to sweat blood through every pore. He wished to cry and roar in utter agony and distress, "Now! Why should I live here? Father into thy hands I commend my spirit".

His head leaned upon his shoulders. The shouting and rejoicing of the soldiers, the lamentations and shrieks of the women as well as the wailing and sobbing of the children echoed and reechoed everywhere on the hilltop.

I feel that tumultuous resounding everywhere on this hilltop! The uproar of the soldiers is drowning in the lamentations of women and children!

*"Let his blood be on us, and on our children!"*

Oh Rulers, Commanders and Protectors of Law, the blood of the righteous who are attacked and killed in their utter helplessness, being too weak to raise even a little finger against injustice, will be on you and on your children. It's the Truth! The truth and the only truth!

Throwing down the inscribed stone, the Wanderer looked up at the sky. His eyes seemed to be wet with his scalding tears.

Whence cometh justice? The uproar of the selfish and the mentally abnormal is increasing! And the lamentation of women and children is lingering around Golgotha!

Whose death is signified by this uproar and weeping? Does it mark the incarnation of the people's savior? But...! Those who take birth in this holy land are mere anti-Christs!

These Saviors, who prove themselves anti-Christs through their words and deeds, and even by their deaths, are actually the deceivers of the people of Judea; they are the betrayers of the virtuous Erewhonians! The biographies of these saviors are mere blasphemy! And the biography of that anti-Christ who took birth in Erewhon has also become a part of history.

The nauseating memory of those art-murderers who abundantly produced the pictures and statues of the anti-Christ in order to be consecrated by the Erewhonians troubled the Wanderer. He spat out his contempt, with a gargling noise. Taking up a sharp chisel, he began to inscribe the blasphemy in history or the gospel of the anti-Christ on a new stone. It had been dictated to the Wanderer by the twelfth disciple of the anti-Christ, just before he had shot himself to death.

Three imported cars sped along the palace-road of the capital city. They stopped with a screech just in front of the parliament building.

From the first car, came out a fat politician, patting his pot belly. From the second car, out came a fat business man, tinkling the money in his pocket. A fat priest came out of the third car, caressing his flowing, grey beard.

Three of them came to the entrance of the parliament building, and called aloud, "Where is she that is born Queen of the Jews?"

The administrators in the parliament building consulted the matter with the palace-astrologers, and said, with the help of a sophisticated computer, "As the King of the Jews was born at Bethlehem, a name beginning with the second letter of the English alphabet, the Queen of the Jews is likely to be born at a place, the name of which begins with the first letter of the English alphabet".

The political leader, the business magnate and the great priest immediately got into their cars and went to the place, the name of which begins with the first letter of the English alphabet. On reaching the place, they saw the child there lying on a royal cot made of sandal-wood, on a bed of foam-mattress and covered by silk clothes, and genuflected before it. *'They presented unto her gifts';* the politician offered gold, the businessman myrrh and the priest frankincense. And they did not return to the capital city, but got into their cars and departed into their own zones of work.

And when Christina was twelve years old, her parents took her to the capital city. She was lost in the crowd, and was found by her parents only after three days' search. They found her in the parliament building, sitting in the midst of the grey-headed politicians, the business magnates and the great priests, *'both hearing them and asking them questions,'* as the Scripture says, on grave political issues! And all who heard her were astonished at her understanding and intelligent answers.

Her parents were amazed when they saw her, and her mother asked her, *"Why did you do this to us?"* And she answered them, *"How is it that you sought me? Didn't you know that I must be about my father's business?"* Later, she went back with them, and was obedient to them, for a few years.

She began her public career by transforming wine into water at a marriage in Cana. Later, on various occasions, she turned those who had good eyesight into blind ones, those who had good-hearing into deaf ones and those who had good oratory into dumb ones. She even transformed the healthy young men into lepers and the healthy young women into those who suffer from bleeding!

At last, when she conspired against and killed her intimate friend Lazarus in a bomb explosion, all the exploiters of Judea, like the politicians, the business men and the priests, joined her company. Out of them, she selected twelve disciples who were genuine scoundrels and slavish sycophants. Seeing her typical activities, a few people distinguished her as the anti-Christ. Yet, they passively watched her progress and popularity, in utter inertia.

The activities of Christina were just like how the majority of the Jews had expected and believed. She captured power and defeated those who were not Jews, in the battle. She tried to prove that she was the Messiah foretold by the prophets in the scriptures. She ruled the country by helping her friends financially and imprisoning her foes cruelly.

Usually thousands and thousands of people gathered at the major grounds and stadiums of the country to hear her *'sermon on the rostrum.'* She distributed meals-packets among them through her disciples, and all of them seemed to be fully satisfied. She not only conveyed her ideas to her disciples and evangelists who gathered at the major grounds of Judea over loudspeakers, but also exhibited them by writing or engraving them on the walls of public buildings.

In the fullness of time for the fulfillment of the predictions, she began to foretell about her own death. Moreover, she had already learnt from history or rather from G. B. Shaw, that martyrdom is the only way by which an incapable person can become famous. And she realized that the people of Judea, who were enslaved by her charming personality and rabble-rousing rhetoric would never make her a martyr!

There onwards, she began making the people of Judea slaves, either through persecution or by creating divisions among them. Through her 'sermon on the rostrum,' she inspired the people by pointing out the importance of sacrificing one's life and of shedding one's blood for the sake of the country. Yet, the people of Judea remained faithful to their Messiah!

When Christina understood that her last days were fast approaching, she asked her disciples to bring a cow and a calf. They brought the cow and the calf and *'put on them their clothes and they set her thereon!'* On her way to Jerusalem, the multitudes, that were before and those that followed, cried, saying, *'Hosanna! Hosanna!'* But, as the fulfillment of prophesy was inevitable, a few of them, forming gangs here and there, began to cry out, 'Away with her, away with her! Shoot her, shoot her!' And at last, her own disciples shot down their Messiah, and the Father Satan's will was done!

Suddenly, *'there was darkness over all the land.'* In order to get light, the people of Judea gave fire to the houses and shops of the innocent citizens of Jerusalem! The graves opened and criminals, sleeping therein arose, and came out in large numbers from the slums and footpaths. They went into the holy city and roamed along the streets, shouting and yelling. All valuable things, including radios, televisions, ornaments and household utensils, disappeared from houses and shops! And the blood that flowed from Golgotha damped the streets of the capital city. Fear and horror spread their wings over the country. Grief and sorrow lingered in the atmosphere!

The death of Christina was just like how she had prophesied! She had declared in a sermon that she was going to offer her blood for the people of Judea, and each drop of her blood would be for her kingdom on earth! Moreover, before her death, she even had foretold that she would come again in another form! And the people of Judea who had lost their wisdom and discretion were waiting for her Second Coming!

Yes! The foolish people of Judea who had lost their wisdom and discretion are waiting, and waiting patiently for the incarnations of evil!

The Wanderer raised his imploring eyes to heaven and his lips trembled with a chant, "Amen; Even so, don't come, Lady Christina! Never! Never again...!"

But the coming of a genuine savior is an inevitability of

history! Only with that Hercules, this Aegean stable can be cleaned! The help of a Hercules is highly needed to break these enslaving chains that tighten the neck every moment, harder and harder.

The people of Judea who lived under the anti-Christ, and the people of China who lived under the First Queen and the people of India who existed under Mohammed-bin Tughlaq are one and the same, the same race and the same people! And similar incarnations of evil may take birth anywhere on this earth, it does not matter whether it is Germany, Italy, Russia, China, Spain, Chile, America, Argentina or Indonesia! Such evil manifestations may implement similar brutalities either directly on their own people or indirectly, through some remote control, on peoples of other countries too! And who knows the master brain behind the juntas, perhaps it is the previous ruler Mr. Jones or it is the future ruler Mr. Pilkington!

The Wanderer remembered that he too was a member of that race of generation caught up in the tightening loops of manacles!

My self too is fettered like Prometheus, and is made a slave to the common fate! Then, the history of Prometheus becomes my own history. His biography becomes my autobiography! Prometheus who always awaits the coming of Hercules!

Yes! I am none but Prometheus! And so, my auto-biography must also be engraved on a piece of granite and be sent to the eternal river Ganges! That strange and mysterious story, in which I, Prometheus, transform myself into Hercules, the invincible Hercules!

The Wanderer cautiously selected a new boulder and began to peck on it...

**P**inned down by the thick manacles and fetters of iron, I have been lying at the steep, eastern-part of that globe-like boulder. Finding no way to escape and seeing none coming to rescue, I have been trying to forget myself in the intoxication of the daily-suffered pain, by seeking consolation in the inescapable Gordian-knot of my own destiny.

Hearing the roar of the waves that rose up from the deep ocean just below my feet, inhaling the nauseating smell of the saline wind that blows hard against my face, fixing my tired eyes in the vacuity beyond the horizon, and tasting the disgusting bitterness of my solitude, I have been waiting for that mirage of freedom and emancipation.

But, as I have been pushing away the moments, one by one, having merely a numbed body and mind that had lost their sensitivity, and being bound by the iron-chains that have been gnawing into the flesh of my limbs, the sound of the flapping wings of vultures that come to peck and eat my liver, drags me back, again and again, towards the bitter reality of my plight.

Those gangs of greedy vultures have been queuing, and desirously awaiting their chance to peck and eat at least a piece of my liver! They are flying towards me, beating their wings of white, green, red, yellow, blue, saffron or black feathers. The crowns they placed on their heads carry certain signs and symbols, denoting the land, the ocean and the sky! In their tumultuous voice, my newly-grown liver begins trembling!

A flock of vultures, who have been bearing the signs of the Swastika, the Cross and the Crescent, hopped towards me and began to peck at my liver, saying in a sweet, sonorous voice, 'Our loving son, Prometheus! The life in this world is always full of sorrows and pain. What's needed is that we must undergo these sufferings and hardships with peace and equanimity. And the success of life always depends on one's patience and sacrifice!"

As I was writhing in pain and torture, they sprinkled water on my body, wiped away my tears and fanned me with their wings. My whole body ached in helplessness. But they simply burnished their bloodstained beaks on the rock, sharpened them and, then, flew away one by one, in search of their next victim!

Then, the next band of vultures hopped towards me and began to peck and feed on my liver! They have been bearing on their crowns the signs of the plough, the yoke, the sickle, the wheel, the hammer and so on. While I was wriggling in utter pain, they consoled me by fanning me with their wings and saying, "Our friendly comrade, Prometheus! We have to learn lessons from the facts of history! And, as you know, history always repeats! When we think of the benefit of the world, in a wide sense, the most important thing is the distribution based on needs! In other words, every day you are getting a new liver and every day our hunger is satisfied! It is true that in this process of distribution, some difficulties will be caused to some people. Even then, can we forget the great motto that 'end justifies means?'

When they too had flown away in search of their next prey; a new gang of vultures arrived, and they began hopping towards me to swallow the rest of my liver! Their crowns have been engraved with signs of the balance, the weights, the measuring scales and the measuring vessels!

With the satisfaction of finishing up the last part of my

liver, they laughed aloud and said, "Our great man, Prometheus! You are the fortune of this world! Just think, how important is the part played by the raw materials for the total existence of this world! Generally speaking, we are sure that the main problem faced by us has always been financial. However, when the organizer is successful in properly utilizing the capital for the stirring-up of the production, all problems are solved. For instance, the more water you draw out from a well, the more freshwater will come into it! Is there any meaning for production, if there is no means for supply? When we get satisfaction by eating your liver, you simply get a new liver! Is it not the so-called socio-economic cultural Revolution we always speak about?"

While various flocks of vultures are flying away from me, one by one, I have been struggling in the chains with unbearable pain and agony! But, by then, the travail for the newly-growing liver has begun in me. The consequences that would fall upon me if I break the chain that keeps me from falling down into the roaring waves of the deep ocean just below my feet frighten me to the core. Hereafter, whatever may happen, neither can I bear this eternal pain nor live without breaking these chains that gnaw into the flesh of my hands and legs.

How long could I live here waiting for Hercules who is powerful enough to relieve me from this sad situation? No longer can I wait, like a fool, for the arrival of an imaginary Hercules! It is better to fall into the waves of the deep ocean and seek some new means of escape that will strike my reason, than living a mechanical life, always in the expectation of an unavoidable agony.

The liver that has newly-grown in me throbs with the power and confidence of Hercules! Every minute, my physical strength and mental power are doubling and re-doubling in me!

When the vultures, being frenzied at the taste of my liver approach to eat my newly-grown liver, when the bell-beat of their wings dissolves in the roaring voice of the waves that mount up from the deep ocean, and when the breaking-sound of the chains among which my hands and legs have been tangled, frightens the vultures and pacifies the briny waves, I feel myself changing into a new Hercules...

**H**ercules is immortal! And no deaths for men like Hercules! For that reason, only a Hercules is allowed to live a life of honor and dignity! Fear is not for Hercules! If it is so, how can I become a Hercules? But were I not a mere coward? Alas!

The Wanderer struck on his forehead with his hand in utter despair and helplessness. His mind was wading through the forest of painful memories! Tears of shame and self-disgust flowed down his cheeks.

I am a sinner; a sinner *more sinned against than sinning!* Otherwise, I would not have run away like a coward, leaving my own mother in the midst of danger and hazards! Cowardice, that's my sin! How can I be freed from that sin? Does my sin fly away in the force of this snowstorm? Whither do my dreams lead me? When will this frenzy-dance of nightmares come to an end?

The Wanderer tried to pull himself together. He brooded

over a plan to vomit away the deadly venom brewing in his mind and to purify himself. He was too confused to recognize the voice resounding in his ears.

Is it the sound of the constantly-blowing snowstorm? Or is it the voice of the angel of death? The sins committed by me are not yet forgiven! It means that I will surely reach hell, after my death! If it is hell, let it be so! For, I cannot run away any more like a coward! *'Cowards die many times before their deaths: The valiant never taste of death but once.'* Hell or heaven, that is quite immaterial...

With an adamant heart, he selected a new piece of granite and began to peck on it. Through a nightmare, which would be a part of his autobiography, he was entering into hell, descending down slowly, but steadily...

I cautiously passed the gate and, placing my firm steps one by one, entered into Hell. I was calm and quiet, and nothing disturbed my equanimity and tranquility of the mind. The porters and guards stared at me. Some of them growled and some others snarled at me. A few among them, being unable to face my piercing looks, trembled with fear. It was for the first time, they were seeing a man like me who dared to enter Hell voluntarily! Leaving behind those gatekeepers and guards, who stood transfixed like statues, I entered into the interior part of Hell.

I roamed here and there in Hell, quite passively watching

various sights there. The human creatures that were writhing in flames! While swimming in the boiling lava, they struggled hard to breathe. Their ear-breaking cries and shrieks echoed in every corner of Hell! Some of them were cursing and accusing themselves! Some others were suppressing their pain and anger by gnashing their teeth and pulling at their hair. Even a few among the guards murmured and growled and hummed in utter distress and disgust!

After seeing all these horrible sights, I climbed up on a fiery dais and laughed aloud. All the human creatures suddenly raised their heads and hopefully looked at me. The watch guards strained their ears to hear what I was going to say. And I said in a clear, loud voice, *"Better to reign in Hell than serve in Heaven!"*

Many of them at first did not understand what I said. But one thing happened! Satan, who was sitting on the fiery throne, jumped up and stared at my face with obvious horror! Once again, I laughed aloud, and carefully observed the reaction of the guards and of the poor human creatures. Their eyes were thirsting for consolation! And I said aloud, "Oh, Ye that suffer untold agonies, I shall console you, I shall save you and I shall rule you!"

"No! No! That's impossible!" Satan shouted, tightening his grip on the throne. He continued, "No! That's unnatural! You can't rule this Hell! This throne is mine! From time to time, I have been ruling this Hell, and nobody has the right to challenge my rule in Hell. It is solely my right and the right of my family."

I asked him, laughing more loudly, "Can't you uplift these poor human creatures?" I continued sternly, "You have all the powers with you. You have all the physical and mental strength. Yet, you cannot rescue them or bring them safe-shore from this deep sea of destitution and eternal misery! Aren't they too sinned like you? Then, why aren't you giving them proper positions in accordance with the intensity of their sins? Didn't you boast in Heaven that you'd protect and safeguard equality and democracy? And now, what did exactly happen to you? Give me your answer. And say it aloud!"

Satan sat on his throne, quite exhausted and paralyzed. He looked at me helplessly and tried to avoid my piercing looks. So I turned my face towards those poor human creatures. They were looking into each other's eyes and were heaving hot sighs! I heard a few among them say, "Oh Hell! What do we hear! Satan stepping down from his throne! That'll never happen! Just impossible! Haven't Satan and the members of his family been the rulers here from time immemorial?"

I looked at them sarcastically. There was no use in accusing these poor, illiterate people! From prehistoric times, Satan and his kinsmen were the rulers here. These people could not even think of another person to rule Hell. And the relatives of Satan were not at all ready for any kind of compromise or inter-cession or concession!

Suddenly, a security guard of Satan walked up to me and whispered in my ear, "See! Satan is actually afraid that if these human creatures were uplifted from destitution and misery, they would capture his throne and occupy it."

I stared at the face of that guard and asked him sharply, "Then, why didn't you oppose Satan, even after realizing this truth?"

He replied with an air of sadness and despair, "What can we do! We are not capable enough to rule! We only know to extend our blind support to those who are born to rule."

I turned towards Satan and stared into his hollow eyes. Strongly gripping the armrests of his throne, he was whispering still, "No! I won't surrender! I'll rule Hell and it's solely my own right!"

"Look here! You fool!" I called out watching his movements. I continued in a roaring voice, "Step down from the throne, as you are incapable of solving the problems of this Hell. As you were born and brought up in a royal family, you cannot understand the sorrows of the poor. Being born with a gold-spoon in your mouth, you always dream of the pleasures of Heaven. But, if you think of bringing here the slavery-based hierarchy of Heaven, you are in a fool's paradise! Sooner or later, a revolt will definitely break out even in Heaven, which you think is a place of happiness and abundance. It would be better if you could step down from this throne and get entrance into Heaven by falling at the feet of God! This is the eve of a revolution in Heaven! This is the right time for you! I am giving you a golden opportunity! Take now a quick decision..."

Satan's lips trembled. He raised his hands and said in a stammering voice, "All these years I worked with the aim of bringing only good for this Hell. All the inhabitants here know me and my family very well. I am toiling day in and day out for the sake of bringing equality, fraternity and liberty inside the portals of this Hell. But my progressive schemes will take some more time to produce their fruits. Till the harvest is reaped, all of you have to wait patiently."

Seeing that his words had a sedative effect on the inhabitants of Hell, he pointed his forefinger at me and, with a new spirit and confidence, continued, "Therefore, these sorts of antisocial elements who raise objections and oppose all the progressive works of Hell must be singled out and banished."

I expected that fetters would fall on me at the very next moment. But Satan was afraid to arrest me, as I was standing in the midst of a large, sensitive crowd that was meticulously watching every movement made by him and me!

I also expected that the human creatures would cry out, "Enough! Enough! Away with your reign! For your progressive schemes will never bear fruits nor will they become successful even if many generations pass." But Satan's mesmeric and magical powers had already closed their mouths. He laughed aloud and looked at me triumphantly.

Regaining my balance of mind, I shouted back at him, "No! You cannot cheat these poor human creatures! You are deceiving your own conscience! You may be able to betray a few people for a short period, but you cannot betray the entire population forever. If you have a bit of self-respect or nobility, step down immediately from that throne…"

"Exactly! What you said is hundred percent correct! No more we want your reign, we are totally fed up with your damned rule," cried some of the guards of Satan who were standing very near to me. What a miracle! The support, it came not from the suffering masses but from the ruler's own guards! I felt really honored!

Their words worked like an elixir on me and I tried to concentrate my vigor and vitality. I knew very well that one can make Satan surrender only through patience and willpower. Once I realized that there were at least a few to stand with me, I felt elated, and I tried to raise my voice against Satan. But unfortunately, I felt my words frozen in my throat. No more could I talk against Satan, I realized. But, still I could work; I could do many things against him.

I took a large flaming ember and with it drew a picture on the golden walls of Pandemonium. The picture showed myself standing triumphantly, my right foot placed on the neck of Satan! Seeing the picture, Satan shook with fear or with excessive wrath. He came down with strong chains to bind me and put me in fetters. But acting quickly, I bound him with his own chains!

Satan wailed aloud and said in a pathetic voice, "Look! If I had self-respect or nobility, I would have handed over the power to you earlier. Now, as I am stepping down from this throne, you must do one thing for me. That is... er.... I wish that someone belonging to my own family shall become the next heir to the throne." He stammered as his lips were trembling. He tried to say some more things but all of them were repetitions of the same thing!

Grinding my teeth, I roared, "Get lost! You and your damned royal family...!" I caught him by the neck and pushed him out of my way. Later, I sent him as well as other members of his royal family towards the poor human creatures, to see their sorrow, grief and despair.

I melted the royal chair of gold. I brought many changes in accordance with the situation prevailing in Hell. Hell was rapidly turning into a model socialist country.

By then, riots and revolts broke out in Heaven! Heaving hot sighs, God himself murmured, "I couldn't conquer Satan and his Hell. But that man! He became successful in it! Nothing happened just like I had expected, for he himself was another God!"

I was least surprised when God himself crossed the gate of Hell and approached me. I frankly told Him that I was not at all prepared for any kind of treaty with Him as long as He promoted slavery. With a trembling voice, God said, "Come, friend! We are all equals. Let us fight together for equality, fraternity and liberty."

Those unforgettable moments marked the beginning of a new relationship based on true love and mutual respect... and the birth of a new era...

The birth of a new era! That is what I always dreamt of! But can I break and hurl away one by one the links of that sin-chain which trails behind me?

The Wanderer was recollecting the past events in his life. Staring at the melting snow of the silvery mountains, he tried to regain power and strength.

Yes! My cowardice has melted away like this snow of the Himalayan ranges! Yet I feel selfishness and insolence following me like my own shadow still!

I had this selfishness and this insolence during my earlier days too. And that's why I ran away and hid among the crowds without caring to rescue my own mother! For that ruddy sin, never shall I get forgiveness! Shall I ever be pardoned?

But for this fall, for this sheer collapse, am I only responsible? Is it by my mistake that this holy land fell into the hands of barbarians? This holy land turns itself into a Hell when her own children become pyromaniacs and homicidal fanatics! In such a Hell, the black necromancers and the red wizards and witches perform their horrible orgies, dancing around the boiling cauldron and singing their weird chants: *Fair is foul and foul is fair.* Hell with these political wizards and witches! Hell with these saffron, yellow, green and white clothed religious sorcerers!

Yes! Here, all evil deeds are considered holy rites! All

the citizens roam here seeking caps that suit their heads and gowns that suit their bodies! And those who sell such caps and gowns are actually ridiculing their foolish customers, always showing their bare teeth!

Had I not seen such a scene somewhere in the streets of Erewhon? A farce that appeared so realistic...?

Digging out an old street-play from the storehouse of scummy memories, the Wanderer began to peck on a new piece of stone...

Scene: The crowded courtyard of a magnificent building in the capital city.

Time: Twenty-nine minutes past the break of dawn.

The Protagonist: The skeleton of a merchant, wearing cap and gown made of multi-colored cloths that fully covered his skull and chest-bones except for his teeth that were tangled in a grotesque smile and his palm and finger-bones with which he invitingly beckoned to the passersby.

Action: The Erewhonian mob gathers around the skeleton of the merchant.

The skeleton of the merchant shouted or rather yelled and said in a shrill voice, "Our country has a great tradition. We cannot separate ourselves from that ancient culture. The same old culture is throbbing in the blood and flesh and bones of each one of us. Therefore, come and buy…! The caps and robes which I sell here will make you true patriots. You can become part and parcel of this old pageant of our country only by wearing these caps and robes! Therefore, come and buy, you, my brothers and sisters…! I can supply to you the caps and robes of varying sizes and colors in accordance with your choice, taste and desire. It's a mission of mine and mine only…"

The pied merchant continued his speech, standing on a raised platform. The masses rushed towards him and crowded around him to buy caps and robes. At last, obeying his command, they all formed into a queue as if they were trapped in a magic circle. Being bewitched by his tempting words, they all began to select caps and robes and the merchant gave them according to their desire, taste and choice, but only after getting proper justification for their exclusive selection.

A man came forward and said to the merchant, "I am a man who intentionally starves to death. Give me a saffron robe and a cap."

The merchant stared at him and asked, "Why do you want to dress in the saffron robe? And why do you starve yourself to death?"

"Don't you know that starving is a holy ritual in our country?" he retorted.

The merchant nodded his head in assent and gave him a saffron robe and a cap.

Then, another man stepped forward and said, "I am a mendicant. Give me a green robe and a cap."

The merchant asked him, "Why do you want to dress in the green robe? And why do you beg for a living?"

"Don't you know that begging is a holy ritual in our country?" he replied.

The merchant nodded his head and gave him a green robe and a cap.

A woman, then, came forward and said, "Hey, merchant! I am a maid of the gods and a whore by profession. Give me a red robe and a cap."

The merchant chuckled and asked her, "Why do you want to dress in the red robe? And why do you sell your flesh?"

She smiled lustfully and said, "Don't you know that prostitution is a holy ritual in our country?"

The merchant nodded his head and sent her away with a red robe and a cap.

Then, another woman stepped forward and said to the merchant, "I am going to commit suicide, by jumping into the pyre of my husband. Give me a white robe and a cap."

The merchant asked her, "Why do you want to dress in the white robe? And why should you commit suicide?"

She sobbed aloud and said, "Don't you know that committing suicide is a holy ritual in our country?"

Nodding his head in assent, the merchant gave her a white robe and a cap.

Again, a man came towards the merchant and said, "I am a man engaged in committing homicides. Give me a yellow robe and a cap."

The merchant asked him with curiosity, "Why do you want to dress in the yellow robe? And why do you commit murders?"

He growled and said, "Don't you know that murdering is a holy ritual in our country?"

The merchant nodded his head and gave him a yellow robe and a cap.

Then, another man stepped forward and said, "Hey, merchant! I am a drug addict. Give me a blue robe and a cap."

The merchant asked him, "Why do you want to dress in the

blue robe? And why do you take drugs like opium and ganja?"

He laughed aloud and replied, "Don't you know that the consumption of drugs is a holy ritual in our country?"

The merchant nodded his head and sent him away giving a blue robe and a cap.

A woman, then, came forward and said to the merchant, "I am a woman who has intentionally become mad. Give me a multi-colored robe and a cap."

The merchant asked her with pretended sympathy, "Why do you want to dress in the multi-colored robe? And why did you become mad?"

She, with a roaring laugh, said, "Don't you know that madness is considered a divine gift in our country? Here, people worship those who dance in sheer madness and frenzy!"

The merchant nodded his head and gave her a multi-colored robe and a cap.

Then, came a man with staggering steps and said, "Hey, merchant! I am a drunkard. Give me a violet robe and a cap."

The merchant asked him, "Why do you want to dress in the violet robe? And why do you drink alcohol?

He replied in a highly intoxicated tone, "Don't you know that drinking is a holy ritual in our country?"

The merchant nodded his head in full consent and sent him away giving a violet robe and a cap.

Then, a man and a woman came forward and said to the merchant, "Oh, merchant! Take back our robes and caps! We have decided to live naked."

The merchant watched them with pretended surprise and asked, "Why do you want to return your robes and caps? And why do you plan to walk naked?"

They replied with an air of seriousness, "Don't you know that nude-walking is a holy ritual in our country?"

The merchant nodded his head understandingly and took

their robes and caps back.

Thus, a number of men and women came towards him and bought robes and caps in different colors and sizes, in accordance with their choice, tastes and desire. All of them convinced the merchant of their typical holy rites and vindicated of their rights over their exclusive robes and caps. Thieves and burglars, those who kidnapped and deformed children, and those who forced them to beg, the eunuchs and those who emasculated others, the rapists and the raped, those who organized suicides, homicides, genocides and infanticides, those who walked on burning embers, those who made pyres for widows, those who wounded their own bodies and those who drank raw blood of animals, birds and human beings, the lazy and the gluttonous - all came towards the merchant and bought their favorite robes and caps, after convincing him of the holy nature of their activities. Meanwhile, it also happened that a number of others returned their robes and caps to the merchant and walked away nakedly, wearing sky as their dress.

The skeleton of the merchant continued his sale of robes and caps without feeling any fatigue or boredom. And, through-out the business, his teeth were tangled in a grotesque smile, a smile that enchanted as well as frightened the masses to the core of their very being.

The Wanderer's face turned ghastly and pale. He sat there like a ghost. And the thin mist was spreading over the face of the valley like a linen shroud.

How disgusting it is to live like an inhabitant of the under-world! This country is merely a ghost-farm and, here skeletons are engaged in the trade of buying and selling secondhand goods! These peddlers will not hesitate even to auction away their own mothers! They deify themselves before the ignorant multitudes. And the foolish masses in their craze for salvation, tumble into the pitfalls made by these disguised guys! What a pity!

Does the theory of an age of competition bring consolation to a true patriot? Here, one lives for oneself, and one's ends and means are entirely one's own business! Then, how could one blame those who commit sins for their own existence? Were I not myself such a sinner who had tightened the grip on power and authority for the sake of my own existence? Can I pull out and throw away the roots of that sin, the roots that have gone deep into my very being, even if this earth is destroyed or even if I get a chance to be reborn in some other unknown planet?

The Wanderer was gradually transfiguring himself into an alien creature of an unknown planet of some distant galaxy, fated to travel in a flying saucer from some corner of this obscure universe and to land unexpectedly on a planet called 'Earth' that had been destroyed probably by radiation many a century ago.

He felt himself feather-light as if he were in space! Yet, his subconscious mind was trying to fathom the depth of his own sin. He selected a piece of granite and started pecking on it like a somnambulist. It would have been a report of the foolish findings of some alien creatures from outer space, an incident that would, perhaps, happen many centuries ahead!

It was after conducting a number of researches and experiments in various galaxies and nebulae of the universe that our spaceship arrived at a planet named Earth under the magnetic control of a star named 'Sun'. The Earth was without form and void and seemed like a planet dilapidated to the core, perhaps, due to some kind of radiation. There had been no sign of life anywhere on the planet. However, as there was prima facie evidence of the presence of some creatures with the capacity to think and act on this planet in some bygone age, we decided to land our spaceship on a diamond-shaped valley of the highest snow-covered mountain on the planet.

There we saw the remains and ruins of an ancient culture and civilization. The relics and fossils were also seen scattered all over the area. We were able to gather much data and information about the planet, Earth, as our scientists, forming themselves into small groups, excavated at some spots, using ultra modern equipment of our planet. And, as cosmonauts, we think that it is our duty to give our planet a firsthand report of our discoveries there.

Our first group, with its equipment for deep excavation, dug a particular area, and found certain square-shaped stones. After studying the signs on those stones, our scientists discovered that a generation of creatures named 'Dravidians' had lived and ruled that particular part of the planet.

Another group of scientists dug out certain plates and pots made of copper. The scientists, who made proper studies on them, found out that a generation of creatures named 'Aryans' had lived and ruled that part of the planet.

Digging at a nearby place, a third group of scientists excavated certain urns and vessels made of brass. We discovered that they had been made during the time when a race called 'Bharatans' had lived and ruled that part of the planet.

Needless to say, our unit of cosmonauts became happier and they began to excavate more vigorously. The more we dug the more things we discovered. We dug out certain household utensils and rectangular-shaped plates made of silver, and gold. Our scientists who tried to decipher the picture writings on them meticulously, came to the conclusion that they had been made by a race of creatures named 'Mughuls' who had lived and ruled that particular territory of the planet.

As we were digging another area of the planet, we found the remains and ruins of a civilization which seemed to be advanced in science and technology. A wing of our scientists was totally surprised when they excavated out a metallic cylinder called Time Capsule made of an alloy of steel and platinum. Inside that cylinder, there were some picture writings which could be read only with the help of our sophisticated microscope. After making proper research-studies on them, our scientists came to the conclusion that a tribe named 'Gandhis' had lived and ruled on that particular part of the planet.

We did not get sufficient time to carry on with a systematic excavation of the planet. As we received the message to return immediately to our mother-planet, we hurriedly collected some specimens of stone and soil from that planet, also the things we had taken out from the ground, and got into our spaceship and returned to our planet. Our scientists hope that by conducting more experiments and researches on the things we collected from the planet called 'Earth', we can find out the causes for the destruction of the planet as well as how and why that planet did become ill-suited or unsuitable for the living beings.

However, the prima facie findings of our scientists show that the autocratic tendencies of certain races of creatures as well as the struggle for supremacy among various tribes of such creatures would have been one of the reasons for the destruction of that planet called 'Earth'.

Let all flying saucers crash and disintegrate! For these voyages in the chariots of fancy and imagination will wipe out even the last trace of humanism and philanthropic attitude in me! It will ruin my sense of duty! 'Fancy cannot cheat so well,' as the poet says. Yet...

The Wanderer sat there, his head bent down with the weight of his heavy thoughts. He felt shame and disgrace at the fate of his country and her people.

Perhaps the annals of the descending ages would be true...! Or some corrupted autocrats might have enclosed a distorted history in Time Capsules. Even so... Does it mean that in between the beginning and the end, there are only a few stages that will survive the test of time? If so, how can you blame an extraordinary man who wishes that the name of his family should remain noticeable in all phases of the history of the world?

Yet... Never should I become a pessimist or a cynic. At any case the situation here in this world is not so unchangeable enough to shatter a person's optimism. Then, why should I be so desperate and feel so dejected?

Of course, the changes in seasons bring rains and drought. But they are quite temporary! And this world will never turn once again to 'without form and void.' The earth will remain as the most beautiful planet in this universe and the man will remain the most beautiful of all creations!

This world cannot turn as dry as you think! It is natural that you may feel confused at the sight of evil-signs! Whenever we see the beginning of drought, we run here and there, in panic and fear! Then the turtles turn silent! And Manu too becomes silent as he fails to hear the voice of the turtles that has already ceased to rise from the fields...

Hey, Manu! I can very well understand your sorrow and grief! You are quite helpless as you wait for the voice of the turtles! Even though your sorrow is a fact of history...

The Wanderer was gradually recovering from the trauma that he had been suffering all these months. He selected a new stone and began to peck on it, the annals of the poor Erewhonian farmers... the story of Manu...

The dry sky that yearns for heavy black clouds! The dried and fissured earth that craves for cold water! And then...

Manu, the farmer, heaved hot sighs, staring at those fishes that writhed and died in the withered brooks! The dried-up and parched paddy fields turned pale and ghastly at the hot winds produced by his heavy exhaling. The grains on the paddy stalk which were the dreams of 'tomorrow' changed themselves into 'frustrations' and they fell down as mere chaffy debris. And the weeds laughed aloud, seeing the fate of those hopeful stalks that yearned to survive in such torridity.

The long but frail hands of the farmer drooped down paralyzed making him powerless even to wipe away the tears that collected in the hollows of his sunken eyes. He, like a tattered scarecrow, sat on the muddy bund of the paddy field, expecting the frenzied moment in which the first rain would raise the refreshing smell of the soil to rejuvenate him and other farmers like him.

When the broken yoke and the tattered plough and the famished oxen made deep furrows in the walls of his heart, he shed hot tears, staring at the fissured and agape paddy fields that were lying extended far beyond the reach of his eyes! And his tears flowed down through the dense forest of his unshaven face, and fell heavily on the distorted and ugly face of earth.

How far is the voice of the tortoise? Perhaps the voice of the tortoise may be a utopian concept! But how far is the voice of the turtle doves? Perchance, it also is a platonic dream?

Manu, the farmer, anxiously looked around him. His eager eyes were scaling and searching among the thick growths of wild plants and brambles and briars. He strained his ears worrying whether the voice of the tortoise was rising from the darkness of those scattered wild growths. But…

The time has been over for the rising of the voice of the tortoise which was born to cover a lifespan that exceeded centuries, by securing its safety under its own hard shell and living silently with the courage of duty and sense of humor and, perhaps, sneering always at the tempo of time!

Alas! Alas! There were only the laughs and roars of the locusts that sought comfort under the cool shades of screw pine groves! The thorny pandanus odoratissmus...!

He cautiously watched the little sparrows that pecked on the charred muddy trails of the brooks, in the hope of getting at least a drop of water. He pitied the lily flowers that were brooding in the lily-bulbs being unable to undergo any kind of evolution! He spat out the salt of his sweat that streamed into his mouth.

Suppressed sobs and sighs unknowingly came out of him as he looked with fear at the fireball that was rising up above his head. Gradually, those sobs and sighs changed themselves into weeping and crying! When weeping and crying rose up from each muddy bund of the paddy field, he realized the truth that he was not alone! And when the weeping and the crying mingled with each other, the zeal that was sleeping in him suddenly raised its hood like a serpent.

He ran with great enthusiasm towards the groves of screw pines and other wild plants! He pulled out the black groves of screw pines that were sucking away the last drops of water from the field. He cut them into pieces and threw them into a pile. His plough upturned the growths of wild plants, brambles and briars. And the locusts that were roosting among them flew away crying aloud. As holy, sacrificial fire was devouring the piles of sliced screw pines and other wild plants, he felt as if he was undergoing a sort of self-purgation. And then watching the bonfire, he laughed aloud, and tried to forget himself.

The ripe, ruddy fireball burned down in the west! And

the heart of the boiling sea began to blaze and fume! The undulating seaweeds writhed and struggled in pain! As the wet sighs of the red sea began to rise up, the face of the sky turned black! The golden fishes that were hiding somewhere in the heavens began to swim, swish and flash, among the black clouds! With great joy and rapture, they began to shed tears! Cold winds made deep furrows in the firmament and through those gaps water streamed down! The paddy fields thrilled at the soft touch of water-drops! The chopped face of earth blushed and her charred lips turned red and rosy! The fresh smell of the black soil began to spread everywhere!

The hands of Manu, the farmer, too rose up actively. Old songs that had undergone changes played about his lips! From the muddy bunds of the paddy field, the forgotten songs rose up with a new spirit! And he began to sing aloud the Song of Solomon:

*For, lo the summer is past, the drought is over and gone;*
*The flowers appear on the earth;*
*The time of the singing of birds is come,*
*And the voice of the turtle is heard in our land.*

The joyous chirping of the sparrows which hopped among the flowering plants and shrubs echoed everywhere! The tortoise broke its mysterious silence! The voice of the tortoise that roamed in and around the cultivated fields! The voice of the turtle-dove rose up together with it. And then, the voice of Manu, the farmer, too was dissolving in that great and rejuvenating voice of Nature!!

Perhaps the voice of the tortoise might be a mirage, an eerie dream that would never be realized! And the voice of the turtle-dove might be as real as this world! Was it only a common difference that existed, between species that fly in the sky and the species that crawl on the land, from prehistoric period onwards! But, oh for the voice of the turtle! The voice of the dove and the pigeon!

Only to hear that voice, did I wander all these years! Now I feel triumphant! For now life has come to the flutes, the flutes deserted somewhere on the hilltop and somewhere on the seashore! They are now emitting the eternal song of peace!

Peace... Slomo... Salaam... Samadhanam...!

The whole world waits for peace! Some say that the end of wars is peace! How funny! A war to end wars! A war to bring peace! Is world peace a mirage? As far as poverty prevails in this world, there will be no peace! Once the problem of poverty is solved, there will be the problem of fanaticism and fundamentalism... a fight for racial, religious, political or linguistic domination! Once physical problems end, mental problems begin! Yes! Tolerance is the key-word for peace! No God can bring peace in this world unless Man learns tolerance. Then the eternal song of peace will rise from every corner of this world. And white doves will fly up in the sky!

What happened here is a glorious revolution. Gone is

the rotten smell of the dead doves, massacred by the white cats! New doves have taken birth from the white feathers of those dead doves! If this is not a glorious revolution, what else is this?

But is this a permanent victory? Will the end of all glorious revolutions be just like the expectations of the revolutionaries? Will those-who-never-dream be turned into mere wanderers? Or will the wanderers be turned into those-who-dream?

The Wanderer felt himself being transformed into a prophet. He began to shiver and tremble in a wild, frenzied mood and dance with the spirit of a fierce devotee of goddess *Kali.* He, like the *Pythia,* the priestess of Delphi, the maiden at the Temple of Apollo the Sun-god, was prophesying the future and fate of a nation! Then, he began to scribble on a piece of stone, the oracle which was obscure even to him!

It was a Sabbath day, a holy day for the Jews. Holy days were days when religious people became more fanatic! The same thing happened on that day too!

A number of Jews came to the Synagogue and worshipped their god, Jehovah. It provoked and blinded other people who belonged to other religions and worshipped other gods or goddesses.

They rushed into the Synagogue with their canes and drove the Jews out of the Synagogue. The frightened Jews ran away from the Synagogue and hid themselves in their huts.

And soon, the Synagogue was turned into a Mosque, a Temple or a Church and they began to worship their gods. Actually they were not Muslims, Christians or Hindus but mere Rationalists. And they sat inside the Synagogue not for worshipping gods, as I understood later.

By that time, I could arrive in front of the Synagogue, Mosque, Temple, Church or whatever it might be. The door of the building remained closed and I looked into it through the keyhole. A film was running inside the building and on the silver-screen, placed on the altar, I saw a feature film.

*"Over the fire, there was a big cauldron, and in that cauldron water boiled. Above the cauldron, somebody fixed a big banner with some writings on it."*

With the bright light of the fire below the cauldron, I read the writings on the banner and understood that they were rules, regulations, dogmas and customs of all the religions.

*"The yellow fire burned brightly, the red cauldron turned black and the green water boiled noisily. Soon, as if in a miracle, the banner broke into two and curled sideways."*

A great sound of shouting and clapping came from the audience. The door of the building opened widely and the people rushed out of it with satisfied faces.

Then, a man, as tall as Bram Stoker's fiendish character Dracula, came towards me and touched on my shoulder with his cane. He asked me in a roaring voice, "What's your name?" I said, *"Ram Mohammed Jesus and what not."*

He laughed aloud and beat me two times on my shoulder with his cane. I kept quiet though I felt his beatings had peeled the skin off my shoulder. Of course, initiation ceremonies were always painful! He stared at me and slowly went out of the place with others. As the film was still continuing, I peeped once again into the building to see its last part.

*"Somebody fixed another banner over the cauldron with no writings on it. The water in the cauldron was not boiling and the fire had already extinguished."*

It seemed like a reel of some dumb-film, and nobody was inside the building to see it. I turned to go home.

On my way back, I saw the Jews returning to their Synagogue to worship their god, Jehovah, for it was Sabbath day, a holy day for the Jews!

It is Time that proves the integrity of prophets and the sanctity of their prophetic utterances. Predictions will be marked and noted in the minds of intelligent citizens, and they will not be surprised when they are fulfilled at unexpected moments. And those who set aside such prophesies as unimportant, just because they are obscure to them, will later regret their folly.

The Wanderer stared vacantly at the misty dawn, blossoming on Kangchendzonga. His frenzied shivering subsided and the oracle came to an end. He tried to become normal by controlling his wayward fancies.

What is happening to me? Is my journey only through

meaningless dreams? Is the revolution I envisaged a sum total of my own hopes and fears? Are my aspirations turning into merely worthless abortive revolutions?

It is true that there is no finality for revolutions. When one revolution ends, another one begins! A new revolution gives some consolation to the man who always yearns for changes! Though he struggles for a new and fresh system, what he gets is merely a faded old system! Just the old wine in new bottles!

But, what helps him to push his life forward is his own imagination, his blind, foolish hope! And as he travels in the chariot of his imagination, he reaches, perhaps, in a state of poverty, slavery and bondage! If so...! Woe betide!

As his legs were freezing in the chill wind that heavily blew from Kangchendzonga, the Wanderer felt himself transformed into that helpless man, who sat quite exhausted on the drenched floor of some dark prison-cell in Erewhon. He remembered that it was from that spot that he began his efforts for the Great Escape to this peaceful slope of the Himalayas, by becoming an unimportant link in that glorious exodus!

Oh! The relaxation of January! The Ides of January may be horrible and full of tension! But relax and start counting the fingers on your right hand! And be prepared to rejoice on the fifth day that comes after the Ides of January!

He selected a big piece of granite and began to peck on it, the story of that Great Escape!

Sitting quite paralyzed in the darkness of the nasty cell, the Wanderer stared at the vacuity, beyond the rusty bars of the prison. He felt that he was actually free, and it was the country of Erewhon lying on the other side of the prison bars, that was the real prisoner!

How did I reach this prison-cell? How was I, who had been roaming quite freely through the streets of Erewhon, found to be here on one turbulent midnight, as if in a nightmare?

Well! In a way, I must be thankful to the Erewhonian authorities! How magnanimously did the authorities deal with my crime of trespassing into Erewhon! Am I not allowed to wander anywhere and everywhere in Erewhon, wearing the gold chains and fetters, like those prisoners whom Raphael Hythloday has seen in Utopia, which were symbols of my honorable, rather dignified crime?

A people who think that the wearing of shackles and handcuffs or chains and fetters, is a matter of pride and prestige! Is there any other country in this world that would respect her criminals this much? Crowds were waiting to greet me, wherever I went! The protectors of the law waited upon my orders! The ministers and political leaders invited me to their mansions and arranged banquets in my honor!

Yes! If this country is not a *'cucumber country'*, what else is it?

A sort of sarcastic smile appeared on the Wanderer's face. He bit his lips till he felt the savor of blood in his mouth. Suddenly dark clouds began to sail on his forehead.

But how unexpectedly misfortune befell me! I had been traveling far and wide seeing, hearing and realizing various facts about Erewhon. And, one fine day, I became a prey to malaria, the *'eradicated'* rather the *'prohibited'* disease of the nation. The temperature of my body shot up and I began shivering and talking in a state of delirium. Was it really Malaria? Scientists say that malaria germs are immortal and, if so, the patient also can attain immortality!

The Wanderer remembered his past days in Erewhon, vividly. The cell was damp and murky. He dearly wished for a glass of water. The hungry stones of the prison stared at him through the darkness of the cell.

How suddenly did the situation change, then? People began to watch me suspiciously. The so-called pillars of society ran away from me. And the officers in charge of maintaining law and order stared at me. Many a time, they surrounded my dwelling place. Many times, I was summoned before a tribunal of physicians and surgeons. Though I was not told what my disease was, the doctors suggested immediate purgation. I was undergoing the experience of Franz Kafka's Joseph K. My neighbors and intimate friends moved away from me. They argued for and against me and my disease!

At last, the protectors of law and order removed my gold fetters and chains, and bound my hands and legs with rusty iron handcuffs and shackles. And in the loneliness of a midnight, without informing anyone else, they brought me here and pushed me into the darkness of this prison-cell.

The rusty iron bars licked the soft skin off the Wanderer's palms. A tigerish grin appeared on his face. Gradually, his grip on the iron bars began to loosen.

Is it an exclusive experience? Or is it just my simple fate? Each and every intelligent patriot suffers the same situation, at least once in a while, in Erewhon! Is there a single citizen in this country, who feels proud of these imprisoned patriots?

Earlier days, a few of them would have felt sorrow at the loss of their dear relatives. But later, when the unexpected disappearance of the intelligentsia became a regular phenomenon, they *too* began to ignore it as a common incident. Just like the situation described by Ross in Macbeth:

*"Where sighs and groans and shrieks that rend the air*
*Are made, not marked; where violent sorrow seems*
*A modern ecstasy."*

Yes! Erewhon was suppressing her bursts of cries at the zenith of her helplessness! The Erewhonians, who had even been deprived of their right to cry aloud, tried to swallow down their grief, in vain. The parents who had lost their children, the children who had lost their parents, the young men who had lost their masculinity, the young women who had lost their virginity, the husbands who had lost their honor and the wives who had lost their chastity, all sobbed silently, sitting inside the dark rooms of their huts and houses. The fathers who were made to see their virgin-daughters being molested, the husbands who were compelled to watch their wives being raped and the brothers who were forced to see their sisters being used for unnatural sexual orgies, all heaved hot sighs, keeping their heads down in utter shame and disgrace!

Even the common people of Erewhon felt that the horrifying face of death was staring at them. Those paralyzed creatures sat timidly in their locked-up rooms, always expecting the khaki-uniformed Satans, who would at some odd second of the silent midnight, knock at their doors with their bamboo-batons and would break them open with the kicks of their horseshoed boots.

Hot tears began to flow down from the eyes of the Wanderer. He tried to suppress his sobs. The grimace on his face became uglier. The memory of those past days choked him.

The jails of Erewhon were overflowing with prisoners! When there was no space left in the cells, the prisoners were sent to the shade of trees and grassy-lawns within the premises of the prison. The jail-wardens knew very well that those unfortunate convicts who were handicapped one way or the other, under the cruel torture of the soldiers, could never manage to get away.

The dead bodies of the murdered convicts were burned to ashes, pouring petrol over them, and the burnt remains of their bodies were used as manure for the coconut trees that were growing in the prison-compound. Were they all convicts? Nay, they were just the accused and the suspects!

The groans and cries and shrieks arising from the stony-cells, could not crush down the thick walls of the prison! Almost all who opposed the barbarian reign in Erewhon were thrown down with broken backbones and shattered limbs, and were waiting for the earliest arrival of the angel of death. For whom even life had become a mirage, the pain and grief would be of little significance! The sad plight of a forlorn generation!

Forlorn! The very word, like a knell, echoed in the ears of the Wanderer as he stood in the dark prison-cell, holding its rusty bars with his tired fingers.

> Why should I undergo all these sufferings? Should my body, mind and spirit be purified of sins only through these extreme punishments? Can these sufferings help my purgation and final amelioration? Escape! That's the only natural remedy! Escape by any means!

His mind chanted constantly. He was not willing to leave his hope even at that last moment. And he, for a second, realized that it was not necessary to feel despair when history repeated itself unconditionally. He knew that the words of the prophets were coming true! Erewhon was, then, Rama, where Rachels were lamenting, and mourning and weeping for their children, *'and would not be comforted, because they were not.'*

The Wanderer remembered for a moment that it would be better to become a sycophant where slavery was considered bliss! He thought about the meaninglessness of the freedom that was gained at the cost of a number of human lives, in a country where people died like the falling of leaves from the trees in the forest, unknown, unsung or unlamented! Only fools could find sense in becoming idealists in a country where the people rejoiced at the sudden death or disappearance of a person, in the hope of getting a share of the latter's food ration! And he remembered the words of Hukum Chand in Kushwant

Singh's Train to Pakistan: the only thing a sane person can do in a lunatic asylum is to pretend that he is as mad as the others and at the first opportunity scale the walls and get out.

Yet, the Wanderer knew very well that he could never justify to his conscience, as he had taken a selfish decision to sacrifice his ideals for the sake of merely saving his own life! In the conflict between reason and conscience, his lips whispered that by-hearted prayer of Tagore, though his heart was throbbing in deep penitence:

*"Where the mind is without fear*
*and the head is held high;*
*To that heaven of freedom, my father,*
*let my country awake."*

Here, there is no place for arguments, no value for conscience and no meaning for philosophical thoughts! What arguments are there for a dead man? What claims can he raise? What conscience is there for him? What philosophy? Here, what really counts is the power of reason, the amount of intelligence! What concerns a citizen is his life and life alone! To live is a primary need and for that, all arguments, fair or foul, all talks about conscience or philosophy, all must be buried deep, deep under the heavy weight of practicability and logic!

The Wanderer, contemplating the pros and cons of the situation, was becoming more and more practical. At last, lying on the pallet of straw, he crossed the Rubicon! He turned every stone to arrange a 'face to face meet' with the authorities of the Musical Bank and the Commercial Bank. Fortunately, he got an opportunity to meet them, and as a result of the subsequent intercession, Mistress Nosnibor handed over the responsibility of rescuing the Wanderer from the jail to her second son.

Mister Nosnibor Junior, immediately, got into a balloon and tried to land in the premises of the prison. But he, who always was timid and thoughtlessly-hurried in all matters, jumped down from the balloon before it touched the ground, and as a result, he fell upside down, his head smashed and he *'burst asunder in the midst, and all his bowels gushed out.'* And ever since, that place has been called Aceldama or the field of blood! What an incredible fate, oh Judas!

With the hope burning in him, the Wanderer looked around for a chance to escape. He noticed the balloon that had ejected Mister Nosnibor Junior out, landing near his prison-cell. He looked at it, quite helplessly, through the casement of the prison.

Miracles should happen for one to escape! Whoever opposed, what must happen will happen at the appropriate time! 'Keiy sera sera!' And the tragedy that befalls certain persons may console even the whole nation! How better if one dies for the sake of all the rest! And when Mister Nosnibor Junior died, the latches of the prisons were loosened and knocked away; the doors and gates were opened wide!

The Wanderer, without wasting a minute to think, dashed out of the prison-cell and jumped into the cradle of the balloon. In the loneliness of that night, he was bidding farewell to Erewhon. Within a split-second, the balloon shot up into the sky, carrying the Wanderer. It slowly floated away, along the blue sky, caressing the silver pieces of clouds.

Below the cradle of the balloon, Erewhon seemed to be like a precious diamond. Neither the wailing nor the hot sighs of the Erewhonians did reach him. The balloon, in which he sailed, passed the hills and plains, crossed the rivers and valleys, and rapidly made its way towards the magnificent and splendid mountain ranges of the Himalayas. Gradually Erewhon faded away and away from him, like the waves of a frightful nightmare!

Every moment, the chillness of the air increased. Under him, the foggy hills and the misty valleys passed. Suddenly, he saw the veil on the face of Kangchendzonga glittering at the rays of the morning sun. Piercing the thick fog, his balloon gradually came down to the land.

When it landed on the lap of Kangchendzonga, where the mountains stood around him as if guarding the valley against the polluted air of Erewhon, a deep sigh of relief and relaxation came out from the Wanderer. The uncontrollable grief of a people who were suffocating under slavery and despair had melted into that hot sigh! Perhaps, it would have been marking the beginning of a new Great Exodus!

What is this loud voice? Is the balloon that landed on this valley bursting out with a big explosion? Or is the chariot of my imagination breaking into pieces forever? Or are the black clouds over the breasts of Kangchendzonga quarrelling and fighting among themselves?

The Wanderer sat there silently, staring helplessly at the virgin snow-covered mountain peaks. The lilt and tone of some carnival songs filtered into his ears! He tried to relax himself, leaning on the side of a big stone. And the glassy morning sun, after an absence for many days, was peeping through the golden peaks of the Himalayas!

Is the month of March so lovely and beautiful? Isn't it unveiling to me a new heaven and a new earth? Some changes have come somewhere! Is the chrysalis, in which I have been hiding all these days, splitting apart? Am I undergoing a metamorphosis, from a mere pupa to a wonderful butterfly?

From a far away spot, from some military camp, the sad mourning sound of the veena, flows out of the radio! What is the mystery behind this sound of the veena that continues for at least ten long minutes? Why does the radio-station transmit such an agonizing *veena-music* while, perhaps, waiting for the latest news? Does it mean that some Prime Minister has handed over the power to some military big-wigs? Does it mean that some President has dismissed some Prime Minister and has taken over the power? Does it mean that some Prime Minister, following a miserable defeat in the election, has committed suicide?

**A** long sigh came out of the Wanderer. His lips trembled in a chant: *Dharma Samsthapanardhayam, Sambhavami yuge yuge...*! What should happen will happen at the appropriate time for the protection of moral values! That eternal chant echoed everywhere on the Himalayan ranges. Together with it, the sound of the rolling stones of history on which his nightmares were engraved, stones that were rolling down and down towards the valley!

Those stones will turn out to be landmarks of history. The lapidary inscriptions may be vague and intangible to a certain extent. But, it is often inevitable to put veils over historical truths! Such veiled truths are easy for the clear understanding of the intelligent. They can make such hidden facts quite permeable to the masses, keeping them always on their toes. They will serve as beacons and warning danger-lights for the sailors and travelers who lost their paths.

And for the fools, there is no use in knowing such truths. In between the intelligent and the foolish, there is a vast majority who live fully satisfied by their pretensions. They are incorrigible, and there is no use in expecting any change in them. They are those who proudly declare that the rabbit they caught has three horns! Then, then is the time, for the coming of incarnations!

The Wanderer's eyes sparkled as if he had discovered a new philosophy! His lips shivered in a song:

> *Be sure, death is not for Butler,*
> *Nor for Swift or George Orwell,*
> *Above the change of time, they are,*
> *Of season, place and language,*
> *For, time to time, they manifest*
> *To retain the world's morale!*

Then his mind was brimming over with a sort of divine peace. His heart throbbed with the intense desire for equanimity. The invigorating mountain breeze was caressing his disheveled hair and tangled beard.

If... if only my wanderings had ended here, and now, itself...! If only the springs of my horrid dreams had dried up forever...! If only the curtain had fallen after the frenzied dancing of my frightful nightmares...!

Yes! That is what I have been ardently wishing for all these previous nineteen months! On the midnight of some day in June, while sleeping in the lap of Goddess Mumbai, I had turned into a Wanderer. I who had never seen dreams, ever since became a slave to dreams, a host of frightful dreams! When nightmares were performing the Canto of *Kirata,* I was quite helpless!

But today, I am free! Before my memory becomes mubilous, I have engraved every one of those nightmares on stones! They have become the corner stones of history so that it is impossible even for time to erase them.

There was a time when I had the zeal to burn down everything. There was the desire to melt everything and to mould up new ones! There was the enthusiasm to cry from house-tops against injustice and to hit on the face of the black laws! But, instead of wasting away that indignation and wrath which bubbled and foamed up inside me, I have been trying, as Anantamurthy's character in Avastha, Govindarayyan said, *to change them into blazing words which would burn into flames in every human heart.* I, personally, have been quite successful in my efforts. When the inscriptions on those stones are purified in the kiln of time, they will undoubtedly, be transformed into precious gems! On that day, those lapidary inscriptions will be properly interpreted for the sake of a better progeny who are ready to devote their lives in the quest of truth. They may belong to a generation that has accepted the advice of Tubby Forrester in Lloyd C. Douglas's novel The Disputed Passage, *"Once a fact is amply attested, you are to accept*

*it, no matter how ugly it is; no matter how much you wish it wasn't so; no matter how violently it collides with what you have previously thought and would still prefer to think."*
Only then shall my birth here be blessed and counted.

Even today, I am happy! Quite satisfied of this birth itself! My nightmares have come to an end. My aim, in coming to this lap of Kangchendzonga is fulfilled. Now, the fate of the Man-who-dreams waits to receive me. Lo!!

Blessed are the ones who never dream, for they gain many a joyful moment in their lives! Blessed also are the ones who dreamed, for they gained many a peaceful moment, as and when their dreams ended!

But woe unto you, who are still dreaming, for pain is piling up in your heart, for despair is stagnant in your brain! You stand wonderstruck at those torrential dreams! But a day is coming, when Time will put an end to the flood of dreams! Watch, therefore, and be ye ready, *for in such an hour as ye think not, that day cometh!* So be patient and wait patiently!

He-who-dreams, or the Wanderer, waited and waited patiently. As days passed, the springs of his dreams began to dry up. First, their force subsided, then their spontaneous flow broke and, finally, they ended forever!

Soon, changes came over him. He stood for a moment dazed like a butterfly that comes out of its cocoon after undergoing metamorphosis. He has already been changed into that old He-who-never-dreams, as if in a second birth. He looked around quite bewildered!

Is my wandering reaching its end? Is it, at last, coming to an end forever? All the dreams and nightmares that had come to me like revelations had been engraved on stones and all those stones had been pushed down along the mountain slopes! Every one of them had rolled down into the valley and had fallen into the stream, at the base of the Himalayas!

And when each one of those stones reaches the wide chest of the Holy Ganges, Goddess Ganga with her divine power will assimilate them into herself. The omnipotent, the omnipresent and the omniscient Ganga! The caressing and consoling Ganga! The Ganga who aroused floods with the tears of the molested Mother! The Ganga who cleansed and healed the wounds of the Mother! The Ganga who chastened the raped Mother! The Ganga, the unwritten history and the eternal truth!

He-who-ceased-dreaming was slipping down to a world of reality. His convalescence was quite sudden. Happiness rippled in his heart for a moment. His heart was whispering: Farewell, you nightmares that never may return! Adieu, you frightful nights that had been lustfully kicking in my brain! Farewell, you horrid sounds that resounded when the frightening unknown figures knocked repeatedly on the locked doors of mind during the lonesome moments of midnights! Adieu, you clop-clop sounds of the horse-hooves that quickened the heart!

Once again his heart turned pacific! The golden rays of the morning sun that came breaking the citadel of darkness, showered consolation on him. His lips blossomed in a happy whisper, "Welcome, fearless minds! Welcome heads that hold themselves high!" But where is that heaven of freedom? Where...?

He looked around in fond hope, as paleness was spreading on his face. A sort of peaceful vacuity was conquering his heart. He withdrew into himself the powers of his five senses and concentrated his mind in deep meditation. Squatting in the lap of Kangchendzonga he began to regain strength and acquire power through rigorous meditation.

Once again came in the spring season! But neither did the birds chirp nor did the flowers bloom. Yet, as the mountain-winds began to blow, carrying the flakes of snow from the Himalayan peaks, the breasts of Goddess Parvathi were overflowing with milk!

Suddenly, enlightenment came to him. Though there was no audible music of the flute, he felt it dissolving in the snow-wind. The curtain had already fallen on all his nightmares, and the Canto of Kirata had finally ended. And the horrible figures that had been performing the fierce cosmic dance of Siva had fallen down tired and exhausted on the stage itself. His sins were cleaned; his penance was over. It was time for a new life and he was well-equipped for it. As Milton says of Lycidas:

*At last he rose and twitched his mantle blue,*
*Tomorrow to fresh woods and pastures new.*

Does here end the absurd search for truth? No! Oh, never!

He returned as Man-who-never-dreams, to know the pulse of reality. He walked down towards his dear mother whom he had once deserted blindly like a prodigal son; his head drooped in shame and disgrace. His heart sobbed:

Mother! My dearest mother! Perhaps, there will be left, at least, a little warmth at those breasts that had once spilled milk to nurture me! Won't I get, at least, a drop of it to rejuvenate me? Won't I get, at least, a spark of fire to stir my soul, to refresh my mind, to invigorate my body, which had been benumbed by the snowstorm?

He walked with firm steps, crossing mountains and valleys, passing hills and streams. Then, a sort of elixir that stirs life with the music of the flute or the life-restoring Mritha Sanjeevani was flowing swiftly through his veins like a Parthian shaft. Yes! 'Do your duty and don't flirt with the fruits of it...'

The divine music of the flute guided him. The saffron sky gave him light and the canopy of green leaves offered him shade. The chants of the Buddhist monks reverberated in the atmosphere. How long could rosaries and prayer-wheels save my mother? No more queries! Do your duty and don't flirt with the fruits of it...

*Karmanyeva adhikarasthe*
*Ma phaleshu kadachana*
*Ma karmaphala hethurbhu*
*Ma sankosthu karmane......*

*And the Wanderer's Saga Remains Unfinished*

# Author's Acknowledgements

Now, having read my novel, not, of course, 'at a sitting' as certain critics 'compliment' pulp literature, dear reader, please do bear with me for a few more words. As a student of literature, I have always been drawn to the skits of Samuel Butler, Jonathan Swift, Thomas More and George Orwell. The vein and form of my novel, *The Haunted Man*, have been to a great extent derived from these renowned masters. Though books are 'bloodless substitutes,' I am extremely thankful to a myriad of writers and their works for making me what I am today. As Tennyson's Ulysses says, 'I am a part of all that I have met,' be it in the form peoples, of places or of books. This novel contains a number of quotes and thematic references to the past masters and contemporary quill-wielders. Many of these echoes have been plucked off from my surrealistic memory and, hence, some of them cannot be properly acknowledged. Therefore, I hereby acknowledge my debt of gratitude to all those authors and their publishers from whose pages this novel has derived its sustenance.

A decade of my wanderings through the length and width of India and my not too short sojourn in the Himalayan Valley gave me an everlasting mine of ideas and a continuous source of inspiration that would last a whole lifespan of a creative writer. Then I was so inquisitive, so idealistic, so enthusiastic and so sensitive that my life in those days was a buoyant experience of 'aching joys' and 'dizzy raptures.' With the exception of a few sentences or paragraphs which I revised or added to it later, this novel was almost wholly conceived and written in that hey-day of my existence. I feel quite satisfied in having been able to solidify that unforgettable past through my first novel, *The Haunted Man*.

I have always been a belated traveler. I wrote this novel during the second half of the nineteen seventies and, though the first draft of it was completed by 1980, I could not bring it to the limelight until I met Professor R.E. Asher. I am highly grateful to Professor Ronald E. Asher, Department of Linguistics, Edinburgh University, U. K., former occupant of Vaikom Mohammed Basheer Chair, Mahatma Gandhi University, Kottayam, for reading my novel word by word, for giving his valuable suggestions and for blessing its first edition with a foreword. For more than a decade, the novel in its type-script form had been in circulation among my fellow-academics, until the library edition came out in 1997, and I am very grateful to them for their critical comments. Then a few literary critics came out with their write-ups, and my sincere thanks are due to them; especially to Professor O.P. Mathur, Banares Hindu University, Uttar Pradesh, India, whose article, *Alexander Raju's The Haunted Man: Emergency in a Palanquin of Dreams*, published in the Journal of Indian Writing in English, Gulbarga (Vol. XXV No. 1, 2007) and Dr. B. Keralavarma, Maharajas College, Kerala, India, whose article, *Humour and History: A Reading of Alexander Raju's The Haunted Man*, published in the Journal of KAFLA Intercontinental, Chandigarh (Vol. X, No. 2, 2003) and republished in STARS, a journal of research published by St. Thomas College, Pala, India (Vol. 4, No. 2, 2003), whose articles are republished in this revised edition of the novel.

Last, but not least, my sincere thanks are due to the publishers; firstly to Mr. N.N. Lalu of Lalu Books, Kottayam, Kerala, India, for bringing my novel debut to light as a hardbound library edition in 1997, the Golden Jubilee Year of India's hard-won independence as well as the twentieth anniversary of the withdrawal of the nineteen months' Emergency declared in India in June 1975; and secondly to Mr. Paul

Rabinovitch of CCB Publishing, British Columbia, Canada, who, after a decade of my novel's first appearance into the limelight, dared to bring out a revised edition of it.

The majority of Indian citizens, who celebrate the Indian Independence Day every year, do not know much about the real suffering of the people under the British Rule or about the real sacrifice of our freedom fighters. However, as one among the so-called 'midnight's children,' I thank the then government of 1975 in giving me an opportunity to get a firsthand experience of a similar situation during that most infamous Emergency Period. Hence, I believe that the dedication of the novel is not inapt.

- Dr. V. Alexander Raju M.A., Ph.D., LL.B.
Kallarackal, Eranjal. Kottayam, Kerala, India – 686 004.
E-mail: dr.alexanderraju@yahoo.co.in

# REVIEW – I

### Alexander Raju's *The Haunted Man*:
### The Emergency in a Palanquin of Dreams
### - By O. P. Mathur*

> *"Be sure, death is not for Butler,*
> *Nor for Swift or George Orwell,*
> *Above the change of time, they are,*
> *Of season, place and language,*
> *For time to time, they manifest,*
> *To retain the world's morale." (p. 152)*

The Wanderer-dreamer who sings the above lines recalls: "On the midnight of some day in June, while sleeping in the lap of Goddess Mumbai, I had turned into a Wanderer. Myself who had never seen dreams, ever since became a slave to dreams, a host of frightful dreams. When nightmares were performing the canto of *Kirata*, I was quite helpless." (p. 152). This brings the work near being a memory-novel with the memories emerging in broken and unconnected dreams and nightmares.

To his symbolic portrait of the Emergency, Alexander Raju has attempted to give a thick coating of the venom of anger and horror and a thinner one of underlying comedy and satire. The narrator-wanderer already in a state of somnambulism left his mother-country to perch on the neighboring slopes of the mountain Kangchendzonga and views what was going on in his country through a thick haze of storm, symbolic of the storm raging in his own psyche through shapes and stories that flashed on the screen of his memory.

For this non-narrative novel, the author has devised a duel

strategy. The narrator underwent an existential quest of the self (pp. 15-16) virtually a split personality – the observer and the wanderer. Though both of them are cushioned in the present, the observer-narrator watches his other self, the Wanderer, actually dreaming and recording his dreams and reflections on pieces of granite and throwing them down the slope to be picked up by posterity. The Wanderer's memory had been so deeply impregnated by the events of the Emergency that he actually seems to relive the past. But as the narrator, he takes an objective view of himself (e.g. P.15) commenting and even apparently going to the extent of talking with his other self (pp. 108-9).

For the Wanderer, though the Emergency is now nowhere in reality, it is deeply embedded in his mind. He, therefore, makes a palindrome of "Nowhere" and calls the India of the Emergency 'Erewhon" – the title of Samuel Butler's novel coming in handy, though it is dissimilar from his motherland in both characters (Jawaharlal Nehru and Mr. Nosnibor, Indira Gandhi and either of Nosnibor's daughters and the absence of any similar events in Butler's novel). Its relevance is only in the palindrome – the "the re-established Erewhon" (p. 17). The land of the Houyhnhnms in Swift's *Gulliver's Travels* or Animal Farm in Orwell's novel are of much greater relevance in which "Beasts rule the men" and other inferior beasts as in Orwell's novel about which Raju comments, "Erewhon is undoubtedly the Animal Farm" (p. 73). *Animal Farm* and *Erewhon* merge into India of the Emergency under the autocratic rule of another Napoleona embodying a number of similarities like hereditary rule and her animal emblems (a pair of bullocks and then a cow and a calf, the emblems of the then ruling Congress Party).

Beastliness predominating in men during the Emergency, with even the police force having been transformed into "a gang of uniformed criminals, rapists, sadists, murderers" (p. 20), animal symbols of the rulers and exploiters predominate – the first one of a pair of castrated and thirsty bullocks 'progressing' by moving round and round, turning the sugar-mill, while the owner is enjoying the sweetness of the sugar-cane juice, the product of my blood and sweat" (p. 25). It is a symbol indicating the fundamentals of the situation, the exploiters and the exploited, which the other symbols in the novel emphasize in different ways.

The ruler is the protector of his people like the parents. But the Mother Hen keeping its chickens under the false belief that they need her nourishing milk, makes them deprive one another of their legs, wings, backbones, beak etc. till they become absolutely helpless. Does it suggest the people being deprived of their rights one by one? There are the exploiters and blood-suckers represented by an alliance between mosquitoes and bedbugs. There is also the White Cat who quietly goes on making meal of the credulous doves who too in league with the rats eat up as much as possible of the farmer's produce (p. 39). The doves have been portrayed as immortal, for new doves arise phoenix-like from the feather of the dead ones. The White Cat is hanged upside down from a pole, but who knows her spirit too may be immortal (p. 45)? The two races of the exploiters and the exploited are eternal and sometimes interchangeable. The immortality of the White Cat may be a sly hint at the re-emergence of Indira Gandhi after the General Elections of 1980.

Another powerful animal-symbol is that of a charming but cruel she-spider (also called in the novel 'spidress' may be on the model of 'tigress'). Some other hints regarding her similarity to Indira Gandhi are more closely pronounced – her family coming from outside, its traditional arrogance indicating superiority, the early death of her mother, her ruling the garden like an autocrat, her laying two eggs, like the Princess of China giving birth to two sons.

The portrait of Napoloeona, a human daughter of Napoleon, a pig behaving like a human being, marks an important transition, providing an opportunity to the narrator-observer to indulge in a long discourse which includes the universal human instinct for freedom leading to change and evolution. The Wanderer also passes on from animal images to the human. The symbolic human image that appears first in his dream is that of the idealistic but whimsical Mohammed-bin-Tughlak who not only orders an impracticable and hence infructuous change of capital, but also the inconsiderate and cruel demolition of huts and slums, reminding us of the infamous bulldozer and the havoc it created during the Emergency.

Another memorable aspect of the Emergency is that of Family Planning, which was made to degenerate into a mindless and cruel campaign for compulsory sterilization regardless of age, marital status or other considerations. For all this the palace doctor is rewarded at the end of the Emergency with involuntary impotence – an unconscious victim of his own medicine.

This makes the dreamer pass on to another related image – eunuchs surrounding a queen, the first Queen of China (like the first lady Prime Minister of India), with the eunuchs as her sycophants. Half of her countenance is radiant with a blissful smile and the other half with threatening look (Indira Gandhi's hair of two opposite colors). The people of China, young and old alike, consider her as their mother and the symbol of their country ("Indira is India and India is Indira"). With none but eunuchs around, the Queen has no option but to enter into a liaison with a servant (Feroz Gandhi, a politician of much inferior status) and gives birth to two sons, with golden spoons in their mouths. But the Queen's displeased father get the servant killed, thus leaving the succession solely for the Princess and her two sons. If we ignore chronology and also a bit of history, the situation is not much different from that of Indira Gandhi's "era with a sort of queen-ism" (p. 93).

The dreamer is so deeply involved in his own dream of the queen that he himself enters into it and becomes her seventh husband after the earlier six, suggesting her cabinet ministers of whom Morarji Desai is the first, are deposed. By now the queen having become too old and cruel in sterilizing the people that they revolt against her and the Wanderer puts her safely inside an improvised tomb, declaring her to be dead. This is an obvious reference to her defeat in the General Election of 1977 with the possibility of her coming out of her 'grave' when the time comes, as it did in 1980.

But the images of the untold and untellable cruelties on women and children continue to haunt the Wanderer. His dream merges with that of the reign of another princess, Queen Christina of the Jews, who was born at a place (Allahabad), the name of which began with the first letter of the English alphabet and who rules the country by helping her friends financially and imprisoning her foes cruelly (a reference to financial scams and imprisonments during the Emergency). The novelist makes a reference to her part in persecuting and creating divisions among the people, especially of Punjab. Riding on her emblematic cow and calf, instead of the Biblical ass, she rides and, as apparently wished by her, attains martyrdom by being shot by her own disciples.

In fact, the recurrence of autocratic despots is almost a law of nature:

> *The people of Judea under the Anti-Christ, and the people of China who lived under the first Queen and the*

*people of India who existed under Mohammed-bi-Tughlak are one and the same, the same race and the same people! (p. 118).*

But a savior is inevitably sent every time like Hercules coming to save Prometheus undergoing the agony of his liver being eaten up by vultures over and over again. In another frightful nightmare the Wanderer enters into Hell and challenges Satan who defends himself on the grounds of his family having the right to rule over Hell. Though having been born and brought up in a royal family he cannot understand the sufferings of the inhabitants of Hell and is only beguiling them with promising schemes. He is forced to yield his throne, and then God himself appears with a proposal to the Wanderer to fight for "equality, fraternity and liberty." The oblique references are to the rule of the Nehru family and the Five Year Plans proving largely infructuous. The end of the rule of the family of Satan, i.e. the Emergency, marks the beginning of a new era in which the restoration of the variegated spectrum of our culture is revealed through the sale of multi-colored robes and caps for every belief or way of life. This sale turns the Wanderer's nightmare into another direction – egoism and bitter competition among the earthlings ultimately leading to the destruction of all life as witnessed by a team of galactic visitors in the Wanderer's dream.

Such cataclysmic times are followed by renewal and regeneration. The novelist is careful in pointing out that even during such periods of despotism the craving and hopes for freedom were not entirely extinct, as in the cases of the laboring bullock hoping for the Spring (p. 26); the feathers of the doves eaten up by the 'immortal' White Cat springing like phoenix into a new life (pp. 44-45), the young ones of the spider killing their own mother for the sake of independence (pp. 49-50), the ungrateful dog Nausea kicking away the affection and comfort of living with a loving family and escaping into the uncertainties of a life of freedom (pp. 54-55); the Black Worms of the love of freedom in the brains of the sheep making them frisk on hearing the eternal music of the flute of the shepherd who too had the Black Worm in his head (pp. 55-60), the arrival Hercules and the defeat of Satan.

In the novel the regeneration is clearly marked by the symbol of the farmer Manu, a universal figure whose name occurs in various forms in quite a few myths of different countries, working amidst the rejuvenating voices of nature and the rationalistic awareness of the unity of the messages of all religions personified in the man named Ram Mohammed Jesus.

It is finally in the lovely month of March, made all the more lovely for the Emergency had ended, and by now released from the prism of his 'Erewhon', the Wanderer has undergone a metamorphosis from a mere pupa to a wonderful butterfly (p. 151). No longer haunted by dreams, he is happy in returning to the world of reality as well as to his motherland. But though the storm, both within him and without, is over, his happiness is not unclouded, for he is no longer a split personality but has become re-oriented and whole, one with his observer-cum-reflective self. His experiences now make him realize that what has been may be again, for time moves in a cyclic pattern and history repeats itself in some form or the other. The Wanderer's saga may recur again and again, may be in different forms, and what should happen will happen for the protection of dharma" (p. 151). A similar conclusion of the recurrence of such periods has also been arrived at in a few other Emergency novels like Arun Joshi's *The City and the River* and O. V. Vijayan's *The Saga of Dharmapuri*. For an individual the only choice left is the selfless performance of his duty, as ordained by the Gita.

In fact, this conclusion has not been reached so suddenly, for while the Wanderer's suffering self was a slave to his nightmares and dreams of short allegoric stories causing melancholic chuckles, his observant self was engaged in trying to weave some sort of pattern out of them – socialistic, rationalistic, metaphysical – finally culminating in the religions. It being hardly necessary to go into 'non-fictive' discourses, sometimes so long as almost to earn the nomenclature of sermons, we can have a look at the structural trajectory of the novel. This non-narrative novel embodies in its dreamily selective visits to the Emergency its quintessential aspects – foolish, whimsical, irrational or repulsively gruesome, into some of which the dreamer also enters, as everyone sometimes does in his dreams. The Wanderer also unconsciously performs a journey from the cowardice of flight to a triumphant return, from a divided self to a whole one, all in his subconscious. The series of dreamy episodes are like pearls in a necklace all tied with some tough threads only occasionally visible. Some of them are hatred of exploiters and a deep sympathy for the exploited, love of freedom and a gradual regaining of his strength and optimism, embodied, for instance, in the plight of the bullock to the dreamer's challenge to Satan and talking of equality to God – ultimately the creation of a new world with the optimism, strength and perseverance of a Manu. The dreams are like the swings of a palanquin from one aspect of Emergency to another, from dream to reality and back – but steadily moving on towards a psychic reorientation of the dreamer. This is symbolized in the different tones of the music heard on the course of this psychic journey.

On the whole, this novel is unique both in its treatment of the Emergency as a part of history and as a fountain of a dynamic variety of psycho-somatic responses shown in it –

perhaps allowing the critic to highlight the comprehensive coverage of Wayne C. Booth's famous concept of the novel ("telling as showing") by referring to his own remark that the "line between showing and telling is always to some degree an arbitrary one." (*The Rhetoric of Fiction*, The University Chicago Press, 1961, p. 20).

*NOTE: The page references, unless otherwise indicated in the paper, are to Alexander Raju, The Haunted Man, written about 1987 (as mentioned in the 'Author's Acknowledgements') but published later by Dragon Publications, Kottayam, 1997. Pages 156. Price: Rs. 200/US $20.*

*Courtesy: The Journal of Indian Writing in English, Gulbarga, Karnataka, India (Vol. XXV, No. 1, 2007, pp. 43 – 48).*

*\*O. P. Mathur, a leading Indian critic, is retired Professor of English, Banares Hindu University, UP, India.*

# REVIEW – II

## Humour and History: A Reading of
## Alexander Raju's Novel *The Haunted Man*
## - By B. Keralavarma*

The history of fiction reveals several options available to a novelist who undertakes to engage his sense of history. He could attempt to recreate the remote charm of a bygone era in the manner of Sir Walter Scott. Or, if his purpose were different, he could emulate Grass and dwell upon the impact of epochal events on the lives of ordinary people. Nothing would prevent him if he were to pooh-pooh things like Shaw used to do. Still another way is to follow in the steps of Shashi Tharoor and subject the past to a reassessment in the light of contemporary history and evaluate present happenings against the backdrop of the past.

In a review of Alexander Raju's The Haunted Man I had touched, in passing, on a unique feature of this novelist's treatment of history. It seems, however, that this remarkable singularity exhibited by the novelist in dealing with an eventful phase of Indian History deserves the above elaboration. It would serve my purpose to point out, instead of completing the catalogue that the technique employed by Alexander Raju is, by and large, peculiar. Rarely has humour been employed as a means of coming to terms with history. It would, perhaps, be wrong to suppose that this technique is used merely for chronicling historical facts. In The Haunted Man it is resorted to as a means of grappling with history, of getting accustomed to the political and cultural milieu the novelist finds himself in and, in a larger sense, of validating his existence in such a climate.

Normally one wouldn't expect to find humour in a person's painstaking efforts to relate himself to the history of his nation, which includes bleak, disheartening patches of monstrous despotism. Humour, sometimes, has a therapeutic effect on those who are shattered by the overwhelming forces of history. We are not unmindful of Grass' gnome-protagonist in Tin Drum who speculates in a high vein of humour on the bizarre circumstances in the dwarf's reminiscences, with the contention that the events recalled are not serious enough on that physical deformity renders him incapable of dealing with things in a serious, mature way. Oscar's frivolity is deliberate in the sense that his comic view provides him a sort of protection (a sense, strangely enough, of superiority) against the combined, debilitating pressures of history and personal life. There is, of course, a major difference between The Haunted Man and Tin Drum i.e. that the latter focuses on the parallel between the chase of private life and the political anarchy of the times, Alexander Raju portrays a lone individual's encounter with the blighting storms that blew across India during the Emergency. But in point of technique there is much in common between the two works, the challenge is, as both the writers seem to have realized, to find a way of avoiding pathos and heroism in facing the overwhelming forces of history. Pathos is unacceptable on the ground of its association with pity, even self-pity. Heroism, understood in the sense of a great reaction against external currents so as to expect of an ordinary person. The problem could be restated in the words of Prince Hamlet: "...to suffer the slings and arrows of outrageous Fortune or to take arms against a sea of troubles." There is a point for us to note in the prince's initial reaction against the calamities, before he begins to brood over the choices mentioned above. The idea of playing the mad man, or better, the buffoon, occurs to him spontaneously. That is a bulwark against psychological destabilization. A man of self respect would scorn to be an object of pity which is what he would become if he were merely to "suffer the slings and arrows of outrageous fortune." As an intelligent man who is aware of his strengths and limitations he rejects the glory of heroism.

There is something of the prince and Oscar in the make-up of Alexander Raju's protagonist. There are moments when he rails against the atrocities committed by rulers. But it is not his wrathful indictment that strikes the readers. It is the air of helplessness, of mournful lamentation over his powerlessness that engages our attention. The protagonist of the novel is a wanderer in quest of peace, of release from harrowing feelings of guilt. That the novel clearly charts the trajectory of this voyage raises it from being what our reader has termed "an episodic non-novel" (printed on the blurb of the first edition of the book). To presume that The Haunted Man is a critique of the brief spell of totalitarianism in the history of India and that its chief interest lies in the stark portrayal through a multitude of episodes of horrors that closed in on the land during that period is to hit wide off the mark. If anything, it is a romance that presents the agonizing process of a psychic re-orientation in a time of crisis. One needs only to consider the structure of the novel to glimpse its organic nature. It takes off with the central character beginning to have dreams and ends with his mind being freed from them. Or we may take a close look at one of the leitmotifs in the novel – that of music. This is how music is described at the outset:

The music of the flute was dissolving itself into that thundering roar of the waves and was slowly vanishing in that commotion. And the Arabian Sea, with a sudden convulsion galloped up, gaped and swallowed the city of

Dwaraka, the capital of the divine king of the Yadavas (12).

In an earlier paragraph, the music is described as "progressing violently." In the middle of the novel music seems to have a strange effect on the tramp. "What attracted him (the Slaughterer) was only the odor of Death in that Music of the Flute" (57). At the end of the novel, after undergoing a metamorphosis the Wanderer returns to his mother-land guided by 'the divine music of the flute.' It does not take long to see the roamer's transformation (from a frightful state of nightmares to one of peace) paralleled in the leitmotif.

It remains for us to explain how the haunted man rids himself of the curse of dreams. Since the novel makes continual excursions into the realm of magic realism, its account of the final stage of the protagonist's passage to innocence is not concrete. Alexander Raju renders the culmination (perhaps, this is not so much a culmination as a temporary halt) of the quest more or less in this way. Living in the world of fantasy, the Wander finds himself in prison for contracting a forbidden ailment – malaria. However, he escapes in a balloon and lands 'in the lap of Kangchendzonga.' Mysteriously enough, he feels as if he were being, in a sense, reborn. The experience is one of blossoming forth into 'a butterfly' from the state of 'a mere pupa.' This transition is significant. In the first place it comes about of its own accord, independently of the will of the haunted man. All that he longs for is liberation from the prison. In the novel it coincides with his liberation from the haunting nightmares. That is to say, his enlightenment does not appear, on the surface to be sufficiently authenticated. We are simply not prepared for this kind of conclusion.

It is not to be inferred, however, from the foregoing argument that the quester's redemption from his unusual malady is suspect. On the contrary, close attention to the text would reveal indications of renewal. Moreover, the state of equipoise he gains would appear to be the result of his own endeavor.

It would be proper to begin our scrutiny of the Wanderer's progress with his flight to Mumbai. The narrative expects us to do so because it begins and ends with flight, the second of which is paradoxically a valiant effort to return to the land forsaken earlier. He clings to Mumbai passionately like one who dreads being hunted out. There is no surprise, then, that he is subjected to an endless chain of dreams. It is the natural fate of those who shirk responsibilities. His first dream surrealistically links music with destruction, and foreshadows widespread violence and carnage. In the wake of such massive torture he makes his second flight – this time to the mountains in the north. Here he is sheltered from the brutality of the guardians of law. Ironically, the physical protection afforded by the serene mountains does not instill peace in his restless mind. He is now remorselessly pursued by enemies of a different kind. It is to be noted that his metamorphosis begins here. He is no longer his usual self. He sheds his personal identity to merge with the toiling, struggling mass of tormented humanity. Here is another instance of paradox. He who turns his back on his fellow men, now, should suffer for them and relive their experiences. Risking repetition I should point out that this second paradox is what initiates his regeneration. Initially he is not equal to facing the outrage committed on the land of his birth. Now, by a strange irony of fate he has to witness all such horrendous acts perpetuated on men in the history of our race. The Wanderer, at this stage, becomes a legendary hero. If nothing else happens, this very act of reliving those bitter experiences would lead to a catharsis, and eventually to his regeneration.

It has already been suggested that what fortifies the Wanderer better than the mountains while exposing his vulnerable mind to all sorts of unnerving experiences is an ability to distance himself from the things contemplated to acquire mastery over them by laughing at them. I do not mean to say that our hero maintains this attitude consistently. There are lapses; but he is quick to regain his detachment. We need only take a quick survey of the episodes to see this fluctuating but steady movement towards psychic health and strength.

One of the ways in which the Wanderer keeps himself aloof while encountering a painfully intense reality is the cast of a thin veil of fantasy over it. The quintessence of the experience remains solidly real; only the characters and the locale looking unreal. In the first dream he sees after reaching the safe solitude of the mountains, one notices a small measure of attitudinal improvement. It is not merely the tone of sarcasm in his relation of the innovations in the state of Erewhon that denotes the progress. Of far greater importance is the element of humor in the narrative. The scene of misery and the reign of criminalism draw forth laughter rather than tears. Contrast it with the abject despair preceding the second flight.

The mode of the fable chosen for highlighting the blood squeezing that goes on all round him, also allows him to exercise self-restraint and chuckle inwardly. The fowls that court death to defeat their antagonists, the farmers, delight the spectator. What the protagonist requires is the right perspective that would enable him to see the folly and absurdity of the ridiculous heroics of the rulers. For a while he keeps up a nonchalance and enjoys watching history unfold before him. But there are setbacks when his focus shifts from the monstrous aberrations of the oppressor to the tragic plight of the victim. Probably his indignation chokes him in such a way that he fails to put two of his narratives in any artistic mould resulting in a raw expression of his wrath. First there is an account of the predicament of the inmates of a citadel. The second episode gives a close up of the atrocities committed by soldiers. This is how the feelings of the Wanderer at this stage are described:

> The Wanderer's face reddened with emotions. Tears flowed out of his eyes. Into some deep thoughts he drowned, his fingers dug into his rough beard.

Soon afterwards he recovers his equanimity and comic sense. Consider the introduction of Christina who, for all practical purposes appears as Anti-Christ. She begins her career by converting wine into water, and by managing to get Lazarus killed in an accident.

The euphoria of having withstood the barbarous perversions of Christina is followed by a relapse into guilt and despair. He miserably fails to guard himself from the vultures (symbolizing exploiters of every hue) which feast on him: "...I was writhing in pain and torture..." His guilt-feelings surface in the following words:

> I am a sinner... Otherwise; I would not have run away like a coward, leaving my own mother in the midst of danger and hazards! Cowardice, that is my sin!

This mood of despondency persists for some time. (I neglect here his ousting of Satan from the throne of Hell which helps lessen the intensity of his grief). The experiences which occur at this stage take the novel to its climax. They also plunge the Wanderer into abysmal depths of despair. The weird vision of the skeleton-peddler selling his fare and the bleak vision of a time when the human race has been annihilated by nuclear holocaust and the grandiose structures erected by man have been raced to the ground, make the lithic-historian sweat and gasp.

Just as enlightenment comes after a dark night of the soul, he resurrects after the fall. The first stirrings of buoyancy spring from his meeting with Manu, the farmer whose optimism, initiative and tenacity infect the Wanderer. One thing that Manu does is particularly instructive. When he sees his land lying devastated by a severe drought he is overcome by sorrow. But he does not yield to the anguish, and does what he can to recover the fertility of the farm. He piles up dry twigs and makes a 'sacrificial' fire. Then, incredibly he 'laughs aloud' watching the conflagration. What appeals to the Wanderer we may presume is Manu's gift of laughing in the face of adversity. It is certain that if there is anyone to whom he owes anything, it is Manu. The pupil learns quickly and finds the fruits of his learning unbelievably sweet. The immediate result of his association with Manu is that he gets elevated spiritually and becomes a prophet. Even when he prophesies a bleak future, he does not lose his self-control. After this there is a moment when he slips backward but he pulls up together to undergo the last of his experiences and enjoy the exhilarating release from the haunting dreams and feelings of guilt and inadequacy. I have said he is liberated from the dreams, but it would be better to look upon them as the means of his regeneration. The experience may have been painful, but in the last analysis, edifying and purifying. Emboldened thus, he returns to his motherland. Our close reading of the text bears out the point that the focus of The Haunted Man is on the psychic reorientation of the protagonist.

*Courtesy: The Journal of KAFLA Intercontinental, Chandigarh, India (Vol. X, No. 2, 2003 pp. 17 - 23) and republished in STARS, a journal of research from St. Thomas College, Pala, Kerala, (Vol. 4 No. 2, 2003 pp. 57 – 62).*

*\*Dr. B. Keralavarma is a Research Guide under Mahatma Gandhi University, Kerala, India.*

# ABOUT THE AUTHOR

Born on April 1st, 1952, in Kerala State of India, Alexander Raju studied in St. Peter's Primary School, Vazhoor, St. Paul's High School, Vazhoor, St. Dominic's College, Kanjirappally and Baselius College, Kottayam. He began his career as a freelance journalist as early as 1974, after completing his higher studies in the Universities of Kerala and Saugar, Madhya Pradesh. Touring almost every nook and corner of India, he acquired a firsthand knowledge of the Indian ways of life among various ethnic groups who differed totally in their culture, religion and language. When Sikkim became the twenty-second State of India, he joined the staff of *Sikkim Express* as one of its sub-editors and later became the editor of *Bullet*, a newsweekly published from Gangtok. He was one among the three-member team that launched *Dainik Aawaz*, the first Nepali News-daily of India.

Returning to his native state of Kerala, he worked as a lawyer for a short while. In 1981, he joined the faculty of English at Baselius College, Kottayam, his own alma mater, as a lecturer. Since 1990, he has been serving as a registered Research Guide in Mahatma Gandhi University, Kerala, India. Currently he is Professor of English in Bahir Dar University, Ethiopia.

Alexander Raju, an Indian English critic, poet, novelist and short story writer, has many books to his credit. *Ripples and Pebbles* (1989), *Sprouts of Indignation* (2003) and *Magic Chasm* (2007) are collections of his poems. His first novel *The Haunted Man* came out in 1997; the second one, *Upon This Bank and Shoal*, came out in 2008. *Candles on the Altar* (1985) and *Many Faces of Adam* (1991) are collections of his short stories. *The Psycho-Social Interface in British Fiction* (2000) is a critical work.

E-mail Alexander Raju: **dr.alexanderraju@yahoo.co.in**